# Pieces of Forever

-A River Falls Novel-

Valerie M. Bodden

Cover design: Ideal Book Covers

Valerie M. Bodden
Visit me at www.valeriembodden.com

## River Falls Series

Pieces of Forever
Songs of Home
Memories of the Heart
Whispers of Truth

## River Falls Christmas Romances

Christmas of Joy

## Hope Springs Series

Not Until Christmas
Not Until Forever
Not Until This Moment
Not Until You
Not Until Us
Not Until Christmas Morning
Not Until This Day
Not Until Someday
Not Until Now
Not Until Then
Not Until The End

# Contents

## *A Gift for You . . .*

Members of my Reader's Club get a FREE story, available exclusively to my subscribers. When you sign up, you'll also be the first to know about new releases, book deals, and giveaways.

Visit www.valeriembodden.com/freebook to join!

*As a young man marries a young woman, so will your Builder marry you; as a bridegroom rejoices over his bride, so will your God rejoice over you.*

—ISAIAH 62:5

# Chapter 1

Most days, Ava could keep the demons of the past at bay.

But today, every click of the shutter reminded her of what could have been.

"Okay." She lowered the camera from her face and studied the model-perfect teenage girl standing in front of the muslin backdrop. Ava had chosen a white background to give the photos an airy, ethereal quality. "Nice job, Harper. Now, can you touch your hand to your face?"

"Like this?" Harper lifted a fisted hand to her cheek as her friend Emily, whom Ava had already done a set of shots for, giggled from behind Ava.

"You look like that statue," Emily said. "You know, the one with the guy all hunched over?"

"The Thinker?" Ava smiled as both girls dissolved into giggles. She'd been fun and silly like this once too. Some days it felt like a long time ago. Other times, like now, those days bit close at her heels. "I was thinking more like this." She lifted her own hand to her face, wincing internally as her fingertips brushed the ridges of skin that puckered her left cheek. How did she forget sometimes that this was what her skin felt like now? What it would always feel like.

She forced herself to keep her fingers there until Harper mimicked the gesture.

"Perfect." She lifted the camera and started clicking again, calling for the girl to smile, then to be serious, then to make the goofiest face she could muster. The secret to great photos, she'd found, was capturing those moments when a subject was off guard, like in the seconds after Harper pulled her goofy face and then broke into a laugh that brought out her best smile of the day.

"Great." She set her camera on the table of gear behind her. "Why don't you girls go change into your next outfits, and I'll get things set up out here."

As the girls scampered off, giggling as wildly as ever, Ava switched from the white backdrop to a black one, then reset the light levels and repositioned her flashes.

All the while, she battled those demons. If life had gone the way she'd planned, she wouldn't be in River Falls, taking photos. She'd be in New York, on the other side of the lens. She'd be the one who was giggling and rushing off to change clothes and soaking up the spotlight.

*But life didn't go the way you planned.*

She shook off the heaviness that tried to hang on her. She had everything she needed—her own business, her aunt, and her dog. She'd decided a long time ago that it was more than enough.

It had to be.

Ava stepped back and surveyed the studio, tapping the smooth right side of her lips.

Something was missing here.

A chair, maybe. Or no—a ladder.

She was pretty sure she still had one among her props. She stepped around her equipment and bustled toward the back room, which served as both prop storage and a makeshift changing area, with two large changing booths off to the side.

When she reached the room, she stopped in the doorway, looking around. Things were strewn helter-skelter—flowers in a pile on one table, fabrics of different hues on another, shelves crowded with wooden blocks and blankets and one of those metal washtubs everyone wanted a picture of their baby in. Scattered among it all were chairs of various shapes and colors, trunks of every size imaginable, old lighting equipment, and a variety of tripods. It was getting to the point where Ava could barely walk through the space. Aunt Lori kept offering to come and help her sort through things, but Ava always declined. She knew that to Aunt Lori, sorting meant throwing away—she'd learned that in fifth grade when Aunt Lori had "sorted" a pile of Ava's paintings right into the garbage can. Anyway, she'd get around to cleaning up back here someday.

And until then, it was always an adventure.

Her eye fell on the ladder sticking out from behind a stack of large blank canvases she had yet to find a use for. Maybe she'd grab a couple of those while she was at it. They might look artistic leaning against the ladder.

"What do you think happened to her?" The voice carried from the dressing stalls, locking Ava in place. "A fire?" She couldn't tell if the speaker was Harper or Emily.

"I think so," the other girl's voice was quieter but still reached Ava. "My mom said she was supposed to be a model or something."

"Wow. You would never be able to tell."

Ava closed her eyes, allowing herself a slow count of five. She'd heard worse. And it wasn't like the girls were trying to hurt her. They thought she was up front.

And they were only being honest.

"Wouldn't you just want to die if that happened to you?"

"Harper!" Emily's voice scolded around a half-laugh.

"Sorry. But you know what I mean. She's never going to have a boyfriend or anything."

"I heard she used to date one of the Calvano brothers. In high school."

"Ooh. Which one? They're all so hot."

"Eww." Emily made a retching sound. "They're *old*, Harper."

"Not that old. The youngest was in my sister's class, and she's only twenty."

"Well, I can't remember which one she dated. But I guess he totally ghosted her after . . ."

Ava's swallow sliced her throat as she backed out of the room, letting the girls' voices fade.

"Joseph," she wanted to say. He was the Calvano brother she'd dated. But she pressed her lips together and silently moved back into the studio.

There, she forced herself to pick up her camera, to double-check the ISO and the aperture, to shoot a test picture and check the white balance.

Forced herself, when Harper and Emily returned in their new outfits, to smile and nod and take pictures that would highlight their unmarred beauty.

Forced herself, when they were done, to hold her head high and say goodbye as they draped themselves over the boys who had come to pick them up.

Forced herself, as she locked the studio door, to remember that she had chosen this. That she had been the one to do the ghosting, not him.

Not that it mattered. If she hadn't pushed him away, he would have run. And she wouldn't have blamed him.

# Chapter 2

It was finally happening.

Joseph sat in his car, staring at the low brick building where he'd gotten his first job when he was fourteen. He'd had to beg Dr. Gallagher for weeks for that job. But finally the old vet had taken pity on him and let him help with cleaning kennels. From there, he'd worked his way up to checking in patients and then assisting the vet with minor procedures. When Joseph had graduated high school, Dr. Gallagher had promised that if Joseph studied to become a vet, he would sell him the practice one day. And now, after eight grueling years of school, River Falls Veterinary was his.

"Holy smokes," he whispered to himself. What if, after all this time, he didn't have what it took? What if he ran the practice Dr. Gallagher had spent forty years building right into the ground?

Something cold and wet pressed to his cheek, and he laughed, patting his Samoyed's soft white ears. The dog was just what he needed to keep himself grounded.

"You're right, Tasha. God's got this. What are we waiting for?"

He opened his car door, patting the roof. He'd been driving the thing for a decade, and he hadn't been sure it'd get him home from Cornell, but it had. Of course, with the loan he'd just signed to buy the practice, this old rust-bucket was going to have to get him through for a while longer.

Tasha zoomed past him, her nose instantly to the ground. Joseph wondered how many dogs had walked through the doors of this building over the years. He pulled out his keychain and grabbed the key that had been on it for less than an hour, taking a deep breath as he turned it in the lock.

This was it.

He pushed the door open and stepped over the threshold into the next chapter of his life.

Inside, everything was exactly the way Joseph remembered it, right down to the magazines in the racks and the paw-shaped treat bowl on the counter. Dr. Gallagher had even left the hideous paintings of cats in tuxedos.

"Maybe we can replace those," Joseph muttered to Tasha. And he knew exactly who he wanted to paint the replacement pictures. Assuming she would give him the time of day.

But for now, he had work to do. "All right," he said to the dog. "Where do we start?"

Four hours later, Joseph had completed an inventory, placed an order for supplies and medications, and surveyed his patient list for next week. Fortunately, Dr. Gallagher had let patients with upcoming appointments know about the transition—and the majority of them had agreed to continue using River Falls Veterinary with Joseph at the helm.

He thanked God again that he didn't have to start over from scratch.

And while he was talking to God . . . *You know how much I want things to work with Ava this time, Lord. Please make it possible. Or at least let her be willing to talk to me.*

"All right, Tasha. Should we call it a day? Go get us both some treats?" At the last word, the dog's upright ears perked.

Of course, since Joseph had just moved into his new house yesterday and hadn't had a chance to get food yet, any treats were going to have to come after a trip to the grocery store.

"Sorry, girl. I'm going to have to drop you off at home first. It's too hot to leave you in the car." After spending the past eight years in New York, it was going to take a while to readjust to the Tennessee heat.

Twenty minutes later, with Tasha safely dropped off at home, Joseph drove past the familiar storefronts that had lined Main Street since he was a boy: Daisy's Pie Shop, Henderson's Art Gallery, the Sweet Boutique, the Book Den. He crossed the bridge over the Serenity River, driving to the outskirts of town, where the grocery store was located. Sweating lightly after the short walk across the parking lot, he ducked gratefully into the air conditioned store.

He reached for a cart just as another hand landed on it.

A female hand, judging by the bright pink nail polish.

"Oh sorry." Joseph pulled his hand back and reached for another cart.

"Joseph Calvano?" The woman's voice was warm and sugary, slightly higher than most, with a taste of the South that he'd missed during his years in New York. It was a voice he would recognize anywhere.

"Madison Monroe." He turned toward her, holding out his hand, but she dove at him in a hug.

He hesitated a second, then lifted a reluctant arm to her back.

"Your daddy said you were coming home," Madison said as she pulled away, her eyes traveling to his shoes, then back up to his shoulders.

"It's nice to see you," Joseph mumbled. The last time he'd talked to Madison had been as he was running out of the prom he'd taken her to.

"You too. We should get together sometime. Catch up. You owe me a dance, you know."

"Yeah. Um—" He'd never had any desire to take Madison to the prom. He'd only asked her because he was upset that the girl he'd wanted to take—the only girl he'd ever wanted to do anything with—had pushed him away. "Sorry about that." He'd never before considered that it might have bothered Madison. She had so many guys falling at her feet, he figured she probably hadn't even noticed.

"I forgive you. On one condition." Madison pointed her perfectly manicured fingernail at his chest.

"What's that?"

"Dinner. Tomorrow night."

"Oh." Joseph's mind whirred. "I'm sorry, I can't. I'm actually, uh, actually . . ." He scratched his cheek, hoping she couldn't tell he was stalling. "I'm actually seeing someone."

Technically speaking, that wasn't one hundred percent true. But he would be seeing someone soon—as soon as he worked up the nerve to ask her. And assuming that she said yes. That counted, didn't it?

"I should have known." Madison studied his face a little too closely. "You always were too good a catch to stay single."

Joseph had no idea how to react to that. The best he could come up with was a strange sound at the back of his throat. He grabbed for an empty cart.

Madison spun her cart toward the produce section. "I'm sure I'll see you around."

Joseph blew out a long breath as she disappeared. He waited a few seconds, then entered the store, making sure to choose a different aisle than the one she'd headed for. Thankfully, he didn't run into her again as he did his shopping.

As he emerged from the store forty-five minutes later, he tried not to be disappointed that he hadn't seen the one woman he really wanted to see. The same one he'd wanted to take to the prom. It would have taken a pretty big coincidence for Ava to be at the store at the same time he was on his first day home. Not that Joseph doubted it could happen—he'd learned over the years that even the seemingly coincidental was in God's hands.

He whistled as he pushed his cart toward his car, letting his eyes rove to the deep green slopes of the Smoky Mountains that wrapped around the town, making River Falls feel cozy and protected and tucked away in its own corner of the world. He turned his head to the north, squinting, even though he knew her house was too far into the ridges to see from here.

"Watch out!"

Joseph yanked his cart to a stop at the shouted warning.

A dark-haired woman glared at him. His cart was only inches from hitting her.

"I'm so sorry." Joseph steered his cart out of the way as he apologized. "I was lost in thought. Wait. Lori?"

The woman's glare didn't ease. "Joseph."

"Hey." He cleared his throat. Wasn't this exactly the kind of coincidence he needed? "So, uh— How are things?"

"Good." The woman crossed her arms in front of her.

Okay. This was not going well. If Lori was this cold with him, what did that say about how her niece would feel to learn that Joseph was home?

"Glad to hear it." He waited for her to ask how things were with him—to give him an opening to say that he was back in town for good. But she remained silent.

Apparently, he was going to have to take things into his own hands. "I just moved back to town. Bought Dr. Gallagher's practice."

Lori gave a short nod.

"Anyway, uh—" Joseph pulled on the neck of his shirt. Had someone cranked up the thermostat on the sun? "How is Ava?"

There. He'd done it.

Lori's mouth tightened, and he resisted the urge to remind her that Ava was the one who had broken up with him.

"She's fine," Lori said finally.

"That's good." He'd been hoping for a little more information than that. But he wasn't sure he should come out and ask if Ava was seeing anyone.

"She has a photography studio."

"That's great—" He grinned at the thought. Ava had always been artistic. He bet she was a talented photographer. "I'd love to—"

"And she's getting married," Lori cut in.

"I— She's— Married?" Joseph gripped the handle of his cart. His world was tipping. "That's—" He choked on the word *great*. He wanted to be happy for Ava. He really did. "Tell her congratulations from me, would you? I, uh— Wow. I should . . ." He gestured vaguely toward his car.

He didn't wait on Lori's response before practically sprinting away from her.

He unloaded his groceries, then climbed into his car and just sat.

Ava was getting married? To someone who wasn't him? How could that be?

He'd been so sure that coming home to River Falls was more than a chance to start his veterinary practice—it was supposed to be a second chance with Ava. A chance to keep the promise he never should have broken—not even when she'd asked him to.

# Chapter 3

"Why do you keep looking at me like that?" Ava set down her coffee cup to confront Aunt Lori.

"I'm not looking at you like anything." Lori picked at an invisible piece of lint on her flower-print scrubs.

Only fifteen years Ava's senior, her aunt was often mistaken for her sister—but she'd raised Ava since Ava was ten. Sometimes Ava thought of her as more of a friend. Other times as a mother figure.

And today she was getting strong mother vibes from her aunt.

"Oh my stars. Yes you are." Ava passed the last bite of her toast to her dog Griffin. The red-haired Vizsla smacked his lips as he downed it in a single gulp. "You're giving me your I-have-something-to-say-but-I-want-to-protect-you-so-I-don't-want-to-say-it look." It was the same look Lori had given her when she'd told Ava her parents had been killed in a car accident sixteen years ago.

Lori's brown ponytail swished as she shook her head. "That's not a thing."

"It is for you." Ava crossed to the back closet to grab her hiking boots. She had no portrait sessions scheduled today, and she was going to take advantage of the beautiful late summer weather to spend the entire day in the woods with Griffin. The dog's toenails clicked as he followed her every movement. Ava carried the boots to the kitchen to put them on. She wasn't going anywhere until she heard whatever it was Aunt Lori was trying to hide from her.

"I saw Joseph yesterday." Lori's voice was guarded.

Ava's heart skidded to a stop, and for a minute her lungs burned as she forgot how to breathe. When she finally remembered to inhale, she raised a hand to her left cheek, covering her scars.

"I– Where?"

"At the store. He bought out Dr. Gallagher's practice."

"Oh." If he'd bought out the old vet's practice, that meant he was back for good, didn't it? Ava knew that had always been his plan. But she'd assumed those plans had changed, along with all the others they'd made together once upon a time.

"Don't worry." Lori stood and patted her shoulder before carrying her coffee cup to the sink. "I'm sure you'll never run into him. I guess that's one of the benefits of not listening to me when I tell you to get out more."

Ava ignored Lori's reproof and breathed a little easier. Her aunt was right. There was almost no chance she'd run into Joseph. The only place Ava ever went in River Falls was her studio. The rest of her time she spent right here at home on the wooded mountainside.

Lori chewed her lip, watching Ava.

"What else?" Ava demanded.

"He asked about you." Lori made a face as if she'd just cleaned out a bedpan.

"I– Oh." Ava's fingers jerked on her shoelaces. Why would he have asked about her? Was it possible he still . . .

*No.* There was no way that was possible, and letting herself think it was would only be asking for heartbreak.

"Be careful, Ava." Aunt Lori's voice echoed the warning Ava had just given herself.

"There's nothing to be careful of." Ava jumped up from her chair and reached for her backpack filled with camera gear.

"I'm just saying. He already broke your heart once."

Ava shook her head. "It was a long time ago." There was no need to correct Aunt Lori's assumption that Joseph had been the one to end things. Not after all this time. Because it didn't change anything, either way.

She could feel Lori's eyes on her as she led Griffin to the door.

"I have to leave for work," Lori said finally. "And then I have . . ." She turned away and mumbled something as she opened the refrigerator to pull out her lunch.

Ava couldn't be sure, but she thought she'd heard the word "date." But that couldn't be right. Aunt Lori hadn't dated once in the sixteen years she'd raised Ava. Though Ava had never really considered that her aunt may have dated before she'd taken on responsibility for raising her. Lori had only been twenty-five then.

She snapped on Griffin's collar. "Sorry. You have a what now?"

Lori turned to face her, defiance radiating from the set of her jaw. "I have a date." She articulated the words carefully, and Ava couldn't help grinning at the rosy tint that colored her aunt's cheeks. She hadn't known Lori was capable of blushing.

Lori pointed a finger at her. "Don't you dare make fun . . ."

"Make fun?" Ava opened the back door. "Who's making fun? I'm happy for you."

Aunt Lori had given up her own life, her own dreams, to raise Ava. She deserved every happiness.

Even the ones Ava knew she herself would never have.

"Don't stay out too late," she joked as she led Griffin out the door.

"I'm still the parent here, you know," Aunt Lori called behind her before the door closed.

Ava laughed and crossed the yard, stepping into the cover of the trees that sloped upward behind the house. Aunt Lori had a date. And Joseph was back in town. She picked up her pace as the trail she cut through the underbrush steepened. The faster she walked, the harder she worked her muscles, the more she strained her heart, the less it would feel, right? The less the name Joseph would whisper through her head. The less his face—always with that goofy smile—would hover in front of her.

By the time she reached her favorite overlook, Ava's breath seared through her lungs—and still she couldn't reconcile herself to the fact that Joseph was home. That he'd asked about her.

Eight years ago, she had told him to leave, told him she didn't want to see him again, and she had meant it.

Or rather, she had meant that she didn't want *him* to see *her* again.

That she couldn't have handled.

She still couldn't. Not when she looked like this.

Her hand came to her face as she worked to slow her breaths.

It didn't matter that Joseph had asked about her. If anything, it only meant she'd have to be extra careful not to run into him.

And like Aunt Lori had said, that shouldn't be hard. Although she supposed she'd have to find a new vet for Griffin. Maybe in Brampton? Fortunately, the dog had just been in for his annual checkup a couple months ago, so she wouldn't have to worry about it for a while.

Vowing not to think about Joseph anymore, she pulled out her camera and snapped on her 28-millimeter lens, then lifted it to her eyes to capture the view of the rolling mountains and valleys that blanketed the landscape in every direction.

But her gaze kept traveling to the river that wound through the nearest valley, the buildings of River Falls nestled along its banks. She squinted, conjuring up an image of the veterinary office downtown, though she couldn't make it out from here.

What was Joseph doing down there right now? Was he thinking about her? Would he try to call her?

He'd left so many messages for her in those first weeks after she'd told him she didn't want to see him anymore. She'd listened to every one of them at first. Read every text. But she'd never let herself call him back. Never let herself reply.

Eventually, it had hurt too much to even see his messages. She'd blocked his number.

She wondered sometimes how long he'd kept calling after that. She wasn't sure if she hoped that it hadn't been too long before he'd given up—or that he'd never stopped.

Ava lowered her camera. Maybe she should photograph a different spot today, one that didn't make her think of River Falls and Joseph. Calling Griffin, she hiked to a lower elevation, where a narrow stream dropped over a series of small waterfalls. She let herself get lost in the familiar rhythm of composing images, of examining the scene in front of her from every angle, of analyzing the play of light and shadow. She was particularly pleased with a shot of the waterfall through a veil of beech leaves. That one she might give Mr. Henderson to sell in the art gallery.

When she'd exhausted every possible angle of the waterfall, she moved to a clearing carpeted with purple mist flowers. She got several shots of the whole clearing before switching out the lens to focus on close-ups of the flowers and the bees and butterflies that hovered over them. Finally, she straightened, forced to acknowledge the grumbling of her stomach.

She pulled off her pack and rummaged for one of the granola bars she always carried.

"Want a treat, Griffin?" she called, glancing around the clearing.

But he wasn't sniffing in the trees at the edge of the clearing as he had been last she'd seen.

"Griffin." She called louder this time. He'd probably wandered into the trees after the scent of a rabbit or a squirrel. Fortunately, he never strayed far from her side.

She listened for the rustling of leaves or the snap of twigs. But aside from the undercurrent of birdsong, the forest was nearly silent.

"Griffin!" She called again, putting more authority into her voice to mask the fear. "Come."

She turned in a slow circle, squinting into the trees surrounding the clearing, her ears attuned to every little sound.

There.

To the west. A low growl, and then . . .

Was that a yip of pain? It was followed by another, then a strange huffing type of noise Ava had only heard once before . . .

The hairs on the back of her neck went rigid, and she took off toward the sound, ignoring the underbrush and branches that swiped at her as she pushed into the forest.

If that was what she thought it was . . .

A louder yip reached her ears and then a sustained whine.

*Griffin.* Her heart was going to break before she got to him.

Ava stopped and scanned the trees, trying to listen over the racket of her own labored breaths.

There.

To her right.

The hulking form of a black bear slashed at something on the ground.

"Griffin," she cried without thinking.

The bear paused, lifting its head and swiveling toward Ava.

"Get out of here." Though her voice shook, it was loud and commanding. "Go on." She slid her bulky camera bag off her back and lifted it above her head to make herself look larger. "Go away. Leave Griffin alone."

The bear let out another huff, then spun and ran off in the other direction.

Ava held her bag in the air until she was sure the bear wasn't going to turn around, then sprinted for Griffin.

Blood coated the dog's fur, and long gashes sliced his side.

She dropped to her knees next to the dog, who let out a low whimper. "I know, boy. It's okay." She slid her backpack on, then tucked her arms under the dog and picked him up, grunting and stumbling a few steps before she got her footing. She should have gotten a smaller dog. "You hang in there. We're going to get you some help. I promise."

But where would she take him?

River Falls Veterinary was out, since Joseph was there. But Brampton was nearly an hour drive. Did Griffin have that long?

She looked down at the limp dog in her arms, fighting to maintain her footing as she carried him down the mountain.

This dog meant everything to her. Was she really going to risk his life to avoid seeing her ex-boyfriend?

# Chapter 4

Joseph ran his hand over the files in the cabinet drawer. Dr. Gallagher had been a great vet. But one thing he had not been—a great organizer. There must be files in here dating back well over thirty years. And much as Joseph hated to think it, most of these pets had to be long gone—unless they were turtles or parrots. What he needed was to hire someone to clean these files out and enter the current ones in the computer. He added it to his mental list of things to do and slid the drawer closed with a sigh.

What he really wanted was to treat his first animal. He double-checked Dr. Gallagher's paper appointment book. He had an appointment with a chinchilla named Chewie first thing Monday morning. Not exactly an exciting first patient, but it would have to do.

He reopened the file drawer. He might as well familiarize himself with his patient's history. He flipped through files, scanning for the last name of Chewie's owner—Conner. His fingers slowed as he reached the names beginning with "Co-." Cobb. Collins. Comay.

His fingers stopped.

Comay?

As in Ava Comay?

He pulled the file out and flipped it open. Sure enough, there was Ava's wild—artistic, she always said—handwriting on the intake form.

"Griffin," the paperwork read. A Vizsla, or Hungarian pointer.

"A sporting dog, huh?" Joseph hadn't had much experience with the breed, though he remembered they were known for their golden-rust coloring. "Looks like he's five years old."

From her spot on the floor across the room, Tasha lifted her head, ears perked.

"Maybe Griffin is due for an appointment," he said to Tasha, whose tail swished back and forth on the tiles. He ran his finger down the records. "Figures. He was just in a couple months ago." Joseph closed the file, then opened it again, scanning the contact information for Ava's phone number. He studied the digits. It was the same number he'd called a million times—which only confirmed his suspicion that she'd blocked his calls long ago.

He stared at his office phone.

That number wouldn't be blocked.

He could call and say he was updating his records. He could hear her voice. Ask how she was.

*And then what?*

She was marrying someone else.

The news still hadn't fully penetrated his brain. How was it even possible? She'd promised Joseph forever—and he'd promised her the same.

Sure, they'd been kids when they'd made the promise. But that didn't mean he hadn't intended to keep it. He'd thought she did too. Until she sent him away.

He stuffed Griffin's file back in the drawer.

*You should have sent the letters.*

Eight years' worth, currently stuffed in an unpacked box in his living room.

What if he got them out now, gave them to her? Would that make a difference?

But he dismissed the idea before it had fully formed.

She was marrying someone else, and he wasn't going to interfere. He cared about her too much for that.

He gave the filing cabinet drawer a hard shove, and it closed with a slam that rocked the whole structure.

Tasha gave him a look that said he was behaving like a child.

"Sorry," he huffed at her.

The dog got up and padded to his side, prancing a little as she always did when she wanted a walk.

"Fine." He rubbed her ears. "I'm not getting anything done here anyway." He could always come in this weekend to finish up his preparations for Monday.

The dog pranced again as he grabbed her leash. "At least you'll never leave me, will you, girl? You're the only one I need."

He flipped off the lights and pulled his keys out of his pocket, then opened the glass door, letting Tasha dart through it ahead of him. As he turned to lock up, the shriek of tires pulled his attention to the driveway just in time to see a silver SUV tear through the parking lot toward the door.

It slammed to a stop only feet in front of him.

Joseph's heart jumped straight to the person inside. That red hair was unmistakable.

Had Ava heard that he was home? Did she want to tell him that it had all been a big mistake? That he was the one she wanted to be with?

Her door flew open, but the moment she jumped out, every thought he had fled.

Blood.

She was covered in blood.

A flash of that night—of the way her skin had been all puckered and blistered and angry—shot through his mind, but he pushed it away. He had to stay focused on right now.

"What happened?" He rushed toward her, his hands going to her arms to check for injuries. "Are you okay?"

"It was a bear." She wrenched away from him and reached for the vehicle's back door. "It got him pretty bad." She yanked the door open to reveal a medium-sized reddish dog stretched across the seat, dried blood matting its fur and fresh blood seeping from lacerations on its side. Its breaths were quick and shallow.

Joseph's heart sank. This was not what he'd had in mind when he'd wished for a more exciting first patient. He'd learned about the potential for wildlife attacks at veterinary school, of course, but that was all in theory. He'd never actually dealt with one.

"You have to help him." Those green eyes he'd never been able to resist pleaded with him.

"I promise. You're sure you're okay? It didn't hurt you?" The thought of Ava facing off against a bear tightened his stomach. He should have been there to protect her. How was he never around when she needed him most?

"It ran away. Please, Joseph. Hurry."

Yes, hurry.

He ducked his head into the vehicle and eased the dog into his arms. "All right, Griffin. Let's get you fixed up." Ava ran ahead of him to open the door, then followed him through the lobby and down the hallway that ran behind it to the surgery suite.

Joseph deposited the dog on the table, then scrubbed in and began to prepare his instruments. "Maybe you should wait out front," he said to Ava. She'd never been great at dealing with blood.

But she remained glued to the dog. "I'm staying with him."

He gave her a long look. But if there was one thing he knew about Ava, it was that once she'd made up her mind about something, there was no changing it.

So he picked up a gauze pad and got to work.

Ava's eyes went from Joseph to Griffin and back to Joseph again. She'd been doing the same thing for the past two hours.

Joseph had sedated the dog, who lay completely still on the table. Ava wanted to ask how Griffin was, if he'd be okay, but she didn't want to distract Joseph. He worked methodically, silent aside from an occasional mumbled, "Good dog," as he cleaned and stitched the wounds. He bit the corner of his lip the same way he always had when he was concentrating.

Something soft rubbed against her leg, and Ava looked down to find the white dog that had been padding between her and Joseph nuzzling its head against her knee. She reached with one hand to rub the dog's ears, taking solace in the silky warmth of the fur. This was why dogs made such good therapy animals.

She continued to scratch the dog's ears as Joseph snapped off his thread, then looked up at her with a tired smile. "That was the last one."

"Is he going to be okay?"

Joseph unwrapped the stethoscope from around his neck and held it to Griffin's chest.

"None of the wounds were too deep, thank the Lord. He should make a full recovery. But I want to keep him overnight for observation."

Ava stroked the dog's side, careful to avoid the freshly stitched wounds. Did Joseph really expect her to leave Griffin here alone?

"Don't worry. I'll stay with him." He'd always had the uncanny ability to read her thoughts.

"Oh, I couldn't ask you to—"

"I'm the vet, Ava."

Right. He wasn't offering to stay with Griffin for *her*. He was doing it because it was his job.

She nodded. If he was going to be here, then she should go. They weren't going to sit up together all night—not like that night on the pier. The night they'd made that promise to each other.

Her fingers went to her cheek.

She could only imagine how relieved he must be that she'd let him off the hook from keeping that promise.

"When can I pick him up?" She had to keep her focus on Griffin.

"First thing tomorrow morning. I'll call you." Joseph opened his mouth like he was about to say more. Instead, he brought a hand slowly toward her face.

Ava flinched, pulling back and turning her head so that her scars were away from him. Her scar-covering makeup did a halfway decent job of making her face look closer to natural, but that didn't mean she wanted him examining it.

"Sorry." But Joseph's hand continued toward her. "You have a . . ." His hand stopped at her hair, and he slid his fingers through it, then held up a twig.

"Oh. Thanks." She stepped back, ducked her head, and gave Griffin one quick pat, then fled into the hallway, forcing herself to walk at a semi-normal pace to the lobby.

The white dog trotted at her side.

"Tasha likes you." Joseph's voice was warm as he followed.

She needed to get out of here. But she couldn't resist crouching halfway across the lobby to give the dog's ears a good scratch. "That's a good name." Tasha's fluffy white tail swished from side to side.

After another second, Ava made herself get up, careful to keep the more disfigured left side of her face from Joseph's view. "Thank you."

He shrugged. "That's what I'm here for."

She nodded and darted for the door.

"And Ava?"

She stopped with her hand on the door but didn't look back.

"You'll have to unblock my number." Joseph delivered the comment nonchalantly, but Ava wondered if there was a trace of hurt under his words.

She bobbed her head once and reached for the door again.

"And one more thing," Joseph called.

This time, she turned to look at him over her right shoulder.

"It's good to see you." Wistfulness lined his smile.

"Yeah." She opened the door. "You too."

# Chapter 5

The reflection in the mirror blinked at Ava as she used a large brush to blend the foundation across her scars and down onto her neck. She'd already applied primer and the green-toned concealer that helped to neutralize the red of her scars. The foundation would help to hide some of the ridges and crevices her face wore from years of skin grafts. She couldn't wait to pick up Griffin—Joseph had texted an hour ago to say that the dog was doing well—but she wasn't going to face Joseph with her scars on full display.

Finally satisfied with her foundation, she added a careful application of contour, blush, and highlighter to make her cheekbones look even, despite the pronounced droop to her left jaw.

When she was done, she sat back, giving herself a critical once-over. Her nose wasn't shaped quite right on the left—courtesy of being burned nearly clear through the cartilage—but she'd never found any way to hide that. Other than that, she looked . . . okay. She certainly wasn't going to win any beauty contests or modeling contracts, but she could at least be seen in public without being called a monster.

It had only happened once—but that was enough. She'd just gotten Griffin, and she was eager to socialize the dog because she planned to train him to be a therapy dog. It was the first time she'd gone outside without the full-face mask that was designed to protect her raw skin from the sun—and before she knew anything about makeup. Griffin had run off to sniff another dog being walked by a little girl and her mom, and Ava had chased him, forgetting for a moment about her scars. But when she'd reached them, the little girl had taken one look at her and screamed to her mother to save her from the monster. The mother had shushed her daughter, looking mortified, but Ava had seen the horror in the mother's eyes too as her gaze fell on Ava's face. The woman may not have said the word monster out loud, but it was clear in her expression.

It was why Ava and Griffin stuck to walking in the woods these days.

She pushed the memory away, donned a pair of jeans and a long-sleeved shirt to cover the burns that traveled down her left shoulder and arm and parts of her leg, then pulled on her tennis shoes and grabbed her keys.

Monster or not, she had a dog to pick up.

But as she approached River Falls, a sick feeling twisted her stomach. It was one thing to see Joseph yesterday, when they were both focused on Griffin.

But how was she going to deal with seeing him today? What if that flood of feelings that she had worked so hard to build an impenetrable safe around managed to find its way out? What if she broke down and told him the one thing she'd promised herself she'd never let him know—that she was still in love with him.

*You won't,* she promised herself. *You can't.*

She pulled into the parking lot of the veterinary office, trying to believe her own words.

She'd go in, grab Griffin, and get out.

And as soon as she got home, she'd research a new vet so she wouldn't ever have to see Joseph again.

Easy enough.

She took a bracing breath and made her way into the building. She was greeted instantly by the click of dog toenails.

"Griffin?" Was he already up and around?

But instead of Griffin, Tasha appeared from the back hallway, her tail wagging as she pranced across the lobby toward Ava. Ava laughed and bent to pet her. "Are you the official greeter?"

"Actually, she prefers chief greeter in charge of sniffing new people."

Ava glanced up to find Joseph leaning against the doorway that separated the lobby from the hallway. He looked tired and a little scruffy, his five o'clock shadow thicker than it had been yesterday. But he looked as good as ever. Better, even. He was still tall and lean, but his shoulders had broadened, and thick muscles peeked out from under the sleeves of his t-shirt.

"Well, it's probably best that she be the one to sniff new people, instead of you."

Joseph laughed, the sound rich and melodious and knocking right up against Ava's ribs.

"I don't know." He took a few steps closer to her. "You always smelled good."

In spite of her best efforts to keep it under control, Ava's heart stepped up its rhythm.

*Remember, come in, get the dog, get out.*

She cleared her throat. "How's Griffin?"

"He's doing well. I'm sure he'd be up and playing already if I let him, but he needs to stay pretty quiet for a couple of weeks to let the stitches heal."

"A couple of weeks?" Ava gaped at Joseph. Obviously he didn't know Griffin very well. The dog was an energy machine.

"I've given him a mild sedative to help keep him calm," Joseph said.

Ava nodded, wondering briefly if a sedative would help with whatever was going on with her heart right now.

Joseph's eyes roved her face, and she angled her head so her left cheek wouldn't be in his line of sight.

"I don't know how to thank you enough."

Joseph covered a gigantic yawn. "I could use a cup of coffee."

She met his eyes. Those blue, blue eyes that had melted her heart more than once. He gave her a soft, gentle smile. No pressure, no hint of wanting anything more than a cup of coffee.

Considering that he'd saved her dog, she supposed a cup of coffee was the least she could do. "What about Griffin and Tasha?"

"They'll be fine here." Still that steady gaze.

She nodded.

"Good." His smile grew. "And maybe a slice of pie. Now that I think about it, I never did have dinner last night."

She laughed and pointed a finger at him. "Don't push it." But she'd buy him a slice of pie—a whole pie, a truckload of pies—to thank him for saving Griffin.

The coffee and pie were good. But being with Ava was better. Looking at her made him feel like a desert that had gone too long without rain. She looked different, of course, but still so, so beautiful. He could tell she was wearing makeup to cover up her scars, but he wished she wasn't. He wanted to see her exactly as she was. Not that it mattered either way. She was still Ava.

Even if she seemed skittish, constantly glancing around at the other customers in the pie shop and covering her cheek with her hand. A dozen times, he'd had to resist the temptation to pull her hand away from her face, to really look at her, to tell her what she seemed not to realize—she was perfect just the way she was.

He took a small sip of coffee, wanting to stretch out this moment with her as long as he could.

Ava shifted as her eyes followed a young couple who breezed past their table. Was she thinking the same thing he was? That not too long ago that had been them? That it could be them again?

But no, *that* he knew she wasn't thinking. She had probably been thinking about her fiancé.

The realization turned the pie in his stomach. What was he doing, trying to get close to her again when she was with someone else?

"How's your family?" Ava had returned her gaze to their table, though she was staring at her fork, not at him.

Joseph let out a breath. It was a safe topic at least. "Benjamin is off at school. Studying to be a chef."

"Oh my stars. How can that be?" Ava gaped at him. "Isn't he like twelve?"

Joseph laughed. "I know. It's crazy how fast time goes, isn't it?" He swallowed, resisting the urge to grab her hand and tell her how much he wanted to make up for the time they'd lost together.

"Anyway—" He forced his thoughts back to the topic of his family. "Asher's doing his park ranger thing. He and Ireland are together again. They're getting married in a few months." He didn't mention that seeing his brother reunited with his high school sweetheart had given Joseph hope that he still had a chance with Ava. "Zeb's still a cop. He and Carly got married like five, six years ago." Another brother living out his future with his high school love. It seemed unfair that it wasn't going to happen for Joseph too.

*It's your own fault for waiting too long. You could have tried sooner, if you weren't such a chicken.*

But he hadn't been a chicken. He'd been trying to respect Ava's wishes.

*Keep telling yourself that.*

"I heard that. I was happy for them." Ava's smile seemed genuine. "What about Simeon?"

"Got married a couple years ago. Grace is married too." Wow. He'd never felt more alone. Almost all of his siblings were off and getting married. And here he was, pining for his ex-girlfriend as she prepared to marry someone else.

"Oh yes. I heard all about that from Aunt Lori." Ava laughed. "Big Titans fan, you know."

Joseph laughed with her. "I remember. She should come by and meet Levi sometime. He's a good guy. He and Grace have a bed and breakfast in Wisconsin, but they visit a few times a year." He still couldn't believe he had a former NFL quarterback for a brother-in-law. But it was true that the guy was incredibly down-to-earth. Though if Grace's stories were to be believed, that hadn't always been the case.

"So that leaves Judah. Any word from him?"

Joseph shook his head, anger building as it always did at the mention of his older brother's name. "Not a peep. Not even when Mama died."

"I'm so sorry." Ava's voice was soft and compassionate. "I wanted to come to the funeral but . . ." Her fingers brushed against his hand for a fleeting second.

But it was enough to reassure him that it was really Ava sitting across from him. It wasn't a dream.

"It's okay. I understand why you didn't." Though Mama's death hadn't been unexpected, it must have brought up all kinds of memories of Ava's own parents' deaths. And as much as he'd wanted her to be there, he wouldn't have her relive that for anything. He still remembered the day her aunt Lori had shown up at school to tell her what had happened. They'd been at recess, and Ava had been called inside. Fifteen minutes later, as the rest of the students were lining up to go back in, he'd spotted Ava emerging from the building, sobs wracking her small frame. He'd wanted desperately to cross that playground and take her in his arms. But he was a ten-year-old boy and she was a ten-year-old girl. And ten-year-old boys didn't hug ten-year-old girls. So he'd gone back to class—and then gone with Dad and Mama to visit her after school. He hadn't known what to say, so he'd just sat next to her in silence.

Much like the silence they sat in now.

He wondered what would happen if he took her hand.

Clearing his throat, he tucked his hands under his legs. "Do you still paint? Because I was thinking . . ."

But Ava was shaking her head, her eyes dropping to the table. "I can't. My hand is too damaged. It's why I turned to photography."

She bent and flexed the fingers of her left hand, massaging it with her right.

Joseph's hand sneaked out from under his thigh, and he had to grab his coffee cup to keep from tracing the raised lines of scars that crisscrossed the back of her hand. His grip on his mug tightened. "Does it hurt?"

Ava frowned, watching her fingers open and close. "The skin is tightening up. It's called a burn contracture. My doctor wants me to have another surgery, and I suppose I'll have to do it one of these days."

He stared at her fingers, still itching to hold them. It'd been one of his favorite parts of dating her. He used to look forward to the end of third period every day, because it meant he could hold her hand on the way to their shared fourth-period class.

Something about her hand caught his eye. "You don't wear a ring." He leaned forward, catching a trace of her jasmine scent that had always seemed at once exotic and familiar to him.

"No. I don't really have any rings. Why?" She pulled her hand back and tucked it into her lap.

He shook his head. What business was it of his if her fiancé hadn't given her a ring? Even if Joseph had spent more time browsing for the perfect ring than was probably normal for a high school senior. Not that he'd been planning to propose right then—but he wanted to know exactly what he was looking for when the time came. It'd never occurred to him that the time might not come.

"So when's the big day?" He tried not to wince as he asked. It was better to rip the band-aid off.

"What big day?" Ava lifted her coffee cup with her right hand, keeping her left in her lap.

Was she trying to spare his feelings? She needn't bother.

"Your wedding?"

She spluttered and slammed her cup to the table, coughing violently.

Joseph scrambled for his napkin and passed it to her. "Are you okay?"

Ava nodded, still coughing, as she wiped up the spilled coffee. When her coughing fit had stopped, she crumpled the napkin and tossed it on her empty plate. And then she just stared at him.

"What?" He didn't mean to sound defensive, but that look of hers . . . "Anyone I know?" He probably should have masked his jealousy a little better than that.

Ava blinked. "Anyone you know, what? What wedding are you talking about?"

"Yours." He rolled his eyes. "I just figured your fiancé might be someone I know. It's a small town. I didn't think to ask when Lori told me—"

"Lori told you?" She gave him a dumbfounded stare.

"Yeah. When I ran into her at the store."

Ava made that strangely adorable tsking noise she'd always made when she was annoyed. "She told you that I'm getting married?"

He nodded, much as it pained him. "I get it. It's been a long time, and—"

"Joseph, look at me." Ava's voice was flat, and Joseph raised his eyes to hers, resisting the urge to tell her she was beautiful yet again.

"Do I look like someone who's getting married?" She slid her fingers over her cheek.

"I– What?" Joseph could only gape at her. What was she saying? That she wasn't . . . "You mean you're not getting married?" Dare he let himself hope?

"No." She gave an ironic laugh and shoved her chair backwards as she stood. "I am most definitely not getting married."

"Oh." Joseph stood too, following as she barreled out the door and down the street. "That's great . . . I mean . . ." He trailed off. She was a dozen steps ahead of him and likely wouldn't hear anything he said. Not that he knew what to say.

*Ask her out, you idiot.*

But his brain seemed incapable of forming the question. And considering that she seemed determined to leave him in her dust, now might not be the best time to ask.

Instead, he met her at the door to his office, unlocking it and helping her get Griffin settled into her vehicle, glad to have something to focus on other than his own confusion.

"Thanks." Ava jumped into her SUV.

"Wait. Ava."

She shook her head but didn't close her car door.

"Did something happen? I mean, were you supposed to get married and . . ." If some jerk had hurt her . . . Joseph tensed.

"I was never engaged, Joseph. I haven't even–" She broke off and reached for her car door, but Joseph intercepted her.

"Why would Lori–"

*That's not the important question.*

But it was too late to take it back.

Ava shrugged. "No idea. I'll see you later." She yanked the car door hard enough that Joseph had to let go.

As she backed out of her parking spot, Joseph was left with the morose thought that he'd never see her again, if she had her way.

But if she wasn't getting married, that meant–

Oh, he was definitely going to see her again.

# Chapter 6

Aunt Lori picked up the empty coffee pot and sighed. "I see you haven't forgiven me yet."

"Nope." Ava kept her eyes on her phone, pretending to read the same article she'd been staring at for ten minutes.

"It's been five days. And I've said sorry like a hundred times. Do you want me to go and tell him I'm sorry too?"

Ava couldn't help it. She had to look up. "Don't you dare."

Aunt Lori grinned, and Ava realized she'd been set up.

But if her aunt would go so far as to tell Joseph that Ava was engaged, who knew what else she was capable of. Ava hadn't been able to make herself go into her studio all week for fear she'd run into Joseph in town and have to explain that not only was she not engaged, but she hadn't had a date in the past eight years—and she didn't expect she ever would again. She wasn't naïve enough to think her appearance mattered that little. Besides, she'd seen the way people—men—looked at her: a combination of curiosity and repulsion.

*Joseph doesn't look at you like that.*

But whatever he thought or didn't think about her scars was irrelevant. Especially after what Aunt Lori had told him.

She covered her face. "It's so humiliating. What could you possibly have hoped to accomplish by telling him I was getting married? Don't you think he would have eventually realized something was up when I didn't actually have a wedding?"

Lori sighed. "I don't know. I just saw him standing there, asking about you like nothing had happened, and I snapped. I wanted him to know what he gave up." She came to stand in front of Ava. "Look, I'm sorry. I just didn't want to see you get hurt again."

Ava sighed heavily. She knew Lori had meant well. And she supposed it was partly her own fault for letting Lori believe Joseph had been the one to end their relationship.

The doorbell chimed, and Ava and Lori both froze, staring at each other. Ava couldn't remember the last time anyone had come to their door.

"Expecting someone?" Lori raised an eyebrow at her.

Ava snorted. "Are you? Your date from the other night, maybe?" Honestly, she'd been dying to ask Lori about that all week, but anger had won out over curiosity.

Lori shook her head, though her cheeks took on a girlish pink just as they had when she'd first told Ava she had a date.

The doorbell rang again, and they both jumped, then laughed together, the sound making the same sweet harmony it always had. Ava's chest eased. She hated being mad at Aunt Lori.

"I'm sure it's for you." Ava gestured toward the door. "I'll be in my room."

As Lori hurried toward the door, Ava carefully disappeared down the hallway. Whoever it was, she didn't feel like socializing at the moment—or ever, really. So different from the pre-fire days, when she'd never hesitated to talk to anyone and everyone.

"Joseph." Aunt Lori's greeting carried from the front door, and Ava froze.

She had checked her phone obsessively ever since she'd torn away from his office on Saturday. But he hadn't called or texted even once.

Not that she was surprised. She'd always known that once he saw the extent of her scars—saw what the fire had done to the girl he'd once called beautiful—he would realize how lucky he was that she'd let him go.

So what was he doing here now?

She touched her hands to her face, thankful that she'd put on makeup today.

"We were just talking about you." Lori's venom-laced comment to Joseph set Ava's feet in motion. Joseph did *not* need to know they'd been talking about him.

"Oh yeah?" Joseph's warm reply came just as Ava reached the living room. His smile landed on her, and she had to stop where she was.

"All good, I hope." He winked toward Ava.

"Well—" Lori started.

"What are you doing here?" Ava cut in.

Joseph's smile didn't falter. He held up a blue and white gift bag. "I came to check on Griffin. And to bring him this."

"I– Oh." Well, if he'd been trying to crack that safe around her heart a little farther open, that was certainly the way to do it. Not that he *was* trying to crack it. Or that she was going to let any of those old feelings out.

"He's in the family room." She turned abruptly, trusting Joseph would follow her. "I have to get to my studio soon, so . . ."

"I'll make it quick." Joseph's voice came from right behind her, and she sped up, but not before his familiar scent—a refreshing mix of lemongrass and mint—could overtake her.

She made herself hold her breath until they reached the family room. "I've been keeping him in his kennel mostly, since otherwise he wants to run around." She stepped toward the kennel, where Griffin lifted his head, his tail thumping hard enough to rattle the metal of his cage.

"Hey, boy. Good to see you." Joseph knelt next to the kennel and eased it open, reaching in a hand before Griffin could get up and launch himself out. “Easy. Good boy.” He stuck his other hand into his bag and pulled out a bone, passing it to Griffin. “These are Tasha’s favorites.”

As the dog chomped the bone, Joseph ran his fingers over the healing wounds.

“Do you always do house calls?” Ava didn’t mean to ask, but Dr. Gallagher had never done them. Maybe this was a new service Joseph was starting.

“Only for my very favorite patients.” He glanced over his shoulder, shooting her a grin that made her heart balloon momentarily.

She crossed to the other side of the room and concentrated on straightening the already perfectly straight picture frames that hung on the wall above a narrow table.

“He looks good.” The kennel door squeaked as Joseph closed it.

“Okay.” Ava stared harder at the pictures, then reached for one above her head that really was crooked, feeling, rather than seeing, Joseph come up next to her. He leaned past her to straighten the frame she couldn’t reach. His nearness sent a shiver up her back, and she scooted to the other side of him so that her left cheek wouldn’t be toward him.

But moving to this side did nothing to keep his familiar scent from toying with her memories.

“What happened to all the pictures of you?” Joseph’s face creased into a frown as he studied the wall. Ava looked at the framed pictures too: mostly landscapes, interspersed with a few pictures of Aunt Lori and Griffin and one or two of her parents—the only way Ava could remember their faces after so long.

She shrugged. “I wanted a place to display my work.”

She felt his eyes on her, but she didn’t owe him an explanation for why she no longer looked at pictures of who she used to be—and never allowed anyone to take pictures of who she was now.

She retreated toward Griffin's kennel. The dog could give her moral support if nothing else.

"These are really good." Joseph looked over his shoulder to smile at her, then turned back to the photos. "Who's this little kid with Griffin?"

"That's Dalton. He was a patient at the Children's Hospital where Griffin and I do dog therapy."

"Griffin's a therapy dog?" Joseph gave the dog an impressed look.

"When he's not wrestling with bears."

"Looks like Dalton likes him."

"He did, yeah." Ava blinked. "He died a few months ago."

Joseph sucked in a breath. "Ava, I'm sorry."

She shook her head. "Thanks." One thing working with the kids at the hospital always did was put things in perspective. There were a lot of kids dealing with a lot worse things than she'd gone through.

"How'd you get started doing that?" Joseph left the pictures and crossed the room to stand closer to her.

Why did he keep insisting on standing to her left? She slid past him and moved toward the picture windows that overlooked the backyard. "There was a woman with a therapy dog who visited the hospital when I was there. We all looked forward to their visits so much. When I came home, I knew I wanted to do that too. It took me a while to convince Aunt Lori to let me get a dog, but I've had him for about five years now. I never realized I could have such a strong bond with an animal."

Ugh. Did that sound weird?

But Joseph's smile was filled with understanding. "I've only had Tasha for a year, and I already feel that."

"Have you ever considered training her to be a therapy dog?"

Wait.

What was she doing? She wasn't supposed to be recruiting Joseph to her own hobbies.

But there weren't enough therapy dogs for all the patients who needed them. If Joseph and Tasha could help . . .

"I don't know." Joseph shuffled his feet. "I tend to be better with animals than people. And Tasha's a little wild."

"She seems like a sweetheart. I'm sure with a little training, she'd be a hit."

"And you could help me train her?" Joseph's eyes landed on her.

Well, she'd pretty much walked right into that one, hadn't she?

Ava looked out the window. "I could probably do that."

"Good. We have a deal." Joseph's footsteps approached the window.

She shuffled to the side so he'd have no choice but to stand to her right.

"That where the bear was?" He pointed up the mountain slope.

She nodded, keeping her eyes focused outside. Not on him. "Up over there, you know where the clearing is . . ." She stopped herself. She didn't need to remind him—or herself—of the picnics they'd shared up there. Of the lazy days they'd spent pointing at the clouds and dreaming of forever.

"Do me a favor and don't hike up there anymore, all right?"

She shrugged. "I'll be fine."

"Ava—"

"Really, Joseph, you don't have to worry."

"What if it comes after *you* next time?" Joseph reached for her shoulder, but she sidestepped his hand.

She bit her tongue before she could say it wouldn't matter. It wasn't like a bear attack could make her face any worse. "It won't."

He gave her a hard look. "Don't go alone at least."

"I don't. I have Griffin."

Joseph crossed his arms and looked pointedly at the dog, who was pathetically trying to lick a patch of stitches on his back that he couldn't quite reach.

Okay, maybe not her best argument.

But who else was she going to hike with?

Aunt Lori was always working—not to mention, she preferred viewing the great outdoors from the comfort of the great indoors, where there was air conditioning.

"Tell you what—" Joseph nudged her shoulder with his. "Tasha has been begging to get out for a hike. How about we go with you, once Griffin is fully recovered?"

"You don't have to do that." She didn't need his pity offer.

"I *want* to. Please." He turned his blue eyes on her, and Ava let out a heavy sigh. She didn't have the willpower left to say no to those eyes. She nodded slowly. He'd likely forget about it anyway.

"Good." Joseph looked satisfied. "And in the meantime, promise me you won't go alone."

The word *promise* rang in her ears. She and Joseph had made a pact long ago that any promise they made to each other they had to keep. So far, she'd only ever broken one promise to him—one she never should have made in the first place.

"Joseph, I'm not going to—"

But his eyes fell on her again.

She shook her head, but the words came out anyway. "Fine. I promise."

"Good." Joseph glanced at his phone. "I have to get to the office. But I'm trusting you to keep that promise."

He was almost to the door when she remembered what she'd wanted to ask him. "How'd you know Griffin's name?"

"What?" Joseph stopped, looking confused.

"When I brought him in last week, how'd you know his name before I told you?"

"Oh." Joseph glanced at the floor for a second, then met her eyes. "I looked up your file."

"Oh." Ava had no idea what to make of that. She walked behind him to the door, then stood staring at it after he left.

So he'd looked up her file—or well, her dog's file. That didn't mean anything. He'd probably looked up every patient's file.

*And memorized every pet's name?*

Whatever. It didn't matter.

*And brought every pet a goody bag?*

She couldn't stop the thoughts.

If she stretched her imagination, she could pretend that Joseph was seeking her out. That he wanted another chance with her.

*Stop*, she ordered herself.

There was no point in getting her hopes up. Even if Joseph did want another chance, it was only because he remembered the girl she had been before. He'd realize soon enough that she wasn't that girl anymore.

# Chapter 7

"Earth to Joseph."

Joseph lifted his head just in time to drop his phone and catch the football spiraling straight for him.

"Nice catch." Zeb chuckled as Joseph tossed the ball back to him. "You up for a game, or what?"

"Yeah. Just a minute." Joseph stooped and picked up his phone, which had fallen on the porch step. Fortunately, the thing was practically indestructible, though its case now boasted a nice chip in the corner.

Oh well. It would still serve its purpose. He glanced again at the short string of texts he'd exchanged with Ava over the past week.

Him: *How's Griffin?*

Her: *He's good, thanks.*

Him, next day: *I'm looking for an office assistant. Have any recommendations?*

Her: N*ot off the top of my head. I'll let you know if I think of anyone.*

Him, two days later: *You're still going to help me train Tasha, right?*

Her: *If you're sure you want to do it.*

Him: *I'm sure.*

That last one had been sent yesterday. He tapped on the message box now, his fingers hovering over the keys. What could he say this time?

Him: *How are Griffin's stitches?*

"Seriously, Joseph. Get your back end over here," Zeb called. "It's gonna be dark soon."

"All right, all right." With one last look at his phone to ensure Ava hadn't responded, he set it on the porch railing, then jogged out to meet his brothers in the large front yard of their father's house. They'd played more games of football out here than Joseph could count.

Back in high school, Ava would often come over after school and stay to watch them. He could almost picture her sitting on the steps now, smiling that special smile she'd always reserved for him, cheering whenever he made a play.

Maybe she would be sitting there again soon.

*Yeah, because things are going so well with your reunion so far.*

He chased away the thought. She just needed time. Soon enough, she would see that they were the same Ava and Joseph they'd always been.

"You got an emergency or something?" Zeb frowned at Joseph.

"No. Not today." Although earlier in the week, he'd had to go to the office in the middle of the night to perform an emergency surgery on a black lab that had ingested a corncob. "Why?"

"Never seen a guy so attached to his phone."

"Oh right. Like you and Carly didn't text every second of the day until you got married."

Zeb smirked. "So this is about a girl?"

"It's– What's about a girl?"

"Your obsession with your phone."

Joseph shook his head, but Zeb laughed. "I'm happy for you, bro. I was starting to worry you'd never move on from Ava."

"What's that supposed to mean?" If Joseph were a dog, he supposed his hackles would be standing on end right now.

"Whoa. Easy." Zeb juggled the football from hand to hand. "Just that the past is the past, and it's time to move on. I mean, you went through all of college and grad school without so much as looking at another—" He broke off, understanding dawning on his face. "It *is* Ava, isn't it?"

Joseph tensed. "And what if it is?"

Zeb held up his hands. "Nothing. None of my business. Just— It's been eight years, Joseph. Don't you think she might have changed since then?"

Joseph took a step closer to his brother, not caring that Zeb had a good two inches on him. "And what is *that* supposed to mean?"

"Hey. Nothing." Zeb set a hand on Joseph's shoulder. "I just don't want you to get hurt again."

"Whatever." Joseph shrugged off Zeb's hand and stepped back. "Let's just play." He jogged toward the rest of his brothers. "Asher, you and me against Zeb and Simeon."

He heard Zeb's exasperated sigh from behind him but ignored it. He didn't know what Zeb had against Ava, but he wasn't going to listen to it.

For the next hour, he played hard, intercepting Zeb's passes and bringing him down a few times. By the time they called it quits, Joseph and Asher were up by a touchdown—and Joseph's body ached in ways he hadn't known were possible. Maybe twenty-six was too old for this.

He jogged back to his phone and picked it up, making a point of letting Zeb see him. Though Zeb was the middle brother, he'd always acted like the oldest—or at least the most demanding. Joseph supposed it served him well as a police officer—just not always as a brother.

He let his eyes drop to his phone, his heart jumping as he spotted the text from Ava: *Griffin is good. His stitches are dissolved.*

It didn't take Joseph more than a moment to text his reply: *Great! How about that hike? Tomorrow?*

# Chapter 8

Ava clicked her phone on, scanned the text from Joseph, then clicked it off again, setting it on the kitchen table in front of her. She'd done the same thing a dozen times in the past half hour. A rousing way to spend a Friday night.

*It's no big deal. Just reply already.*

Except, what was she supposed to reply?

A yes was too dangerous. The way she hadn't been able to stop thinking about his visit last week, the way she couldn't stop checking her phone for messages from him, had made that clear.

But saying no seemed unreasonable. First, because she'd promised him she wouldn't hike on her own. And second, because she couldn't come up with a good excuse. Anything she thought of, he would see through.

"What should we do, Griffin?" she murmured to the dog curled up fast asleep at her feet. Now that his stitches were dissolved and she didn't have to keep him cooped up in his kennel all the time, he seemed to be sticking extra close to her. The dog let out an excited yip in his sleep, and Ava rolled her eyes. She was not taking that as an answer.

She clicked the phone on again, letting her thumbs hover over the keyboard. She would say . . .

The sound of the front door opening made her jump and let out a sigh of relief at the same time. Any excuse to delay this decision was welcome.

Griffin jumped up from his spot at her feet and let out a half-bark.

"Nice guard dog work there, buddy." Ava patted his head and pushed back from the table, making her way to the living room to greet Aunt Lori.

But she froze at the threshold of the room. It wasn't only Lori who was standing there. Behind her aunt stood a tall, thin man with the slightest hint of gray in his dark hair. Something about him was familiar, though it took Ava a moment to realize what it was.

"Mr. Germain?" She gaped at her high school history teacher. What was he doing here? With Aunt Lori?

"Hello, Ava." Mr. Germain's voice had always had a warm, friendly tone to it. Ava had often wondered if that was part of the reason so many of her friends had had a crush on him. She was suddenly grateful she hadn't been one of them as she realized why he was standing in her living room.

Mr. Germain was Aunt Lori's *date*.

She blinked from one to the other as Lori closed the door. "I'm going to go put this in the fridge. Unless you want it?" Lori held up a small carryout box. "It's from the Depot."

The Depot? That was a pretty fancy place for so early in a relationship.

"I'm good, thanks." But Ava got the distinct feeling Lori wasn't listening to her, since she'd already turned back to Mr. Germain.

"Can I get you something to drink, Michael?"

*Michael?* Ava snickered to herself. This was too surreal.

"Sweet tea would be perfect, but don't go to any trouble if you don't have any."

"It's no trouble."

Whoa. That smile Lori gave him—Ava had never seen her aunt so . . . so . . . smitten.

Lori squeezed Ava's arm as she passed. "I was just telling Michael about your photography. I'm sure he'd like to see some of your work."

"Very much." Mr. Germain stood at ease, hands in his pockets, as if he'd hung out here plenty of times. The same way he'd always seemed so comfortable standing in front of a classroom, bringing history to life.

"Ah. Sure, Mr. Germain. Most of them are in here." She led him toward the family room.

"Call me Michael, please." Mr. Germain laughed as he followed her. "You haven't been my student in a long time."

Ava nodded, even though there was no way she could call him by his first name. That would be way too weird.

"So, um, these are some of my pictures." As she stopped in front of the wall Joseph had been admiring the other day, she tried not to picture the way he'd smiled at her, the way he'd talked to her as if nothing had changed—when everything had.

It took a moment to realize she'd missed a question from Mr. Germain. "Sorry, what was that?"

"I was just asking if you'd ever consider coming into the school to mentor our yearbook club. We have a few promising young photographers, but I feel like they could use more direction than I can give them."

"Oh. Uh— I—" Her mouth went dry. There was no way she could ever walk into her old high school again. No way she could endure the stares of the students. "I don't think—"

Aunt Lori bustled into the room, balancing three glasses of sweet tea. She passed one to Michael and one to Ava, who took it gratefully, swallowing a long drink to avoid discussing Mr. Germain's question further.

"Should we take this out to the deck?" Lori asked, gesturing toward the French doors that led to the deck Ava had decorated with fairy lights.

Ava gaped at her aunt. She was pretty sure Lori had never voluntarily spent a moment outdoors in her life.

"That sounds perfect." Mr. Germain smiled at Lori, who raised an eyebrow at Ava. "Join us?"

"Oh. Um. I have to . . ." She raised her phone vaguely in front of her.

"It was nice to see you, Ava." Mr. Germain still seemed to think this whole thing was entirely normal. "Promise you'll think about it."

Ava nodded. She supposed there was no harm in thinking about it—since she knew she would never change her mind.

She slipped down the hallway to her room as Mr. Germain escorted Lori outside.

A strange sense of loneliness washed over her as she set her tea down. Aunt Lori had always been the biggest constant in Ava's life—the one who was always there.

Somehow, it had never occurred to Ava that that might not always be the case. If Aunt Lori and Mr. Germain got married, what were the chances they'd want Aunt Lori's grown niece living with them?

"Looks like it's going to be just you and me, Griff."

She glanced at the phone in her hand, then opened to Joseph's text and tapped out a reply.

# Chapter 9

Joseph grunted as he grabbed the backpack he'd loaded with a picnic for today's outing. He was more than a little sore from last night's football game with his brothers, but nothing was going to stop him from hiking with Ava. He whistled for Tasha, but she was already at his feet.

"You're as excited about this as I am, aren't you girl? A little sweet on Griffin maybe?" He scratched behind Tasha's ears, but she dashed for the door.

He chuckled. "All right. I don't want to wait any longer either."

The forty-five minutes he'd waited for her reply to his text last night had been agonizing. But so worth it when he received her tepid, "Sure." His whoop had drawn a look from Zeb that he'd chosen to ignore. His brother didn't know the first thing about Ava.

*And you do? It's been eight years.*

He pushed the question aside and let Tasha charge out ahead of him. Of course he knew Ava. They'd always known each other better than they'd known themselves. He stashed his backpack in the trunk, opened the back door for Tasha, then jumped into the driver's seat. It was going to be a perfect day—the start of everything, he could feel it.

He pressed his foot to the accelerator as he drove out of town, watching his speed closely as he passed the spot he knew his brother liked to sit in his police cruiser. The one and only time Zeb had pulled him over, he'd let Joseph off with a warning—and a promise that the next time he'd get a ticket.

But Zeb's car wasn't at his favorite speed trap.

Joseph pressed harder on the accelerator as the car started the climb toward Ava's house.

Instead of responding with a surge of power, the vehicle quieted as the radio cut out abruptly, and the cold air blasting from the vents vanished.

Joseph flicked at the radio and the temperature controls. But nothing happened, and the car seemed to be slowing down. He pressed harder on the pedal, but the speedometer showed his speed rapidly decelerating.

Behind him, a car horn blared, and a second later, a pickup roared past, horn still screaming.

"Sorry, buddy," Joseph muttered, pulling hard on the steering wheel to move to the gravel shoulder. Fortunately, the car made it all the way to the side of the road before it gave out completely.

Joseph sat staring at the dashboard. Now what?

He tried turning the key in the ignition again, but the engine was silent.

"Okay." He let out a long, slow breath.

First things first. He grabbed his phone and tapped Ava's number. He wasn't going to let her think he'd stood her up.

Using his shoulder to press the phone to his ear, he reached across the passenger seat to dig the owner's manual out of the glove box. He and this car had been through a lot together—and this little book had seen them through most of it.

After paging through the book for a moment, Joseph pulled the phone away from his ear. It should be ringing by now.

No bars.

Joseph groaned and glanced out the window. He'd forgotten how bad cell reception was here.

He tried dialing Dad's number, on the off chance it would work.

But he knew it was futile even before he was met with silence again.

He shoved the phone into his pocket and turned back to the book. But the answer he found there wasn't reassuring—it sounded like an alternator problem. He wasn't a car guy by any stretch, but even he knew that without the alternator, his battery couldn't hold a charge. And he couldn't go anywhere.

All right, then. He clipped Tasha's leash to her collar and got out of the car. "Looks like we're going for a little run before our hike."

They set off back toward town at a brisk jog, but between his sore muscles and the fact that veterinary school hadn't left him much time to run, his pace felt more like a crawl than a sprint. At this rate, he'd get back to River Falls by sometime tomorrow.

And he'd need another shower.

He grimaced and forced himself to pick up the pace.

By the time he'd been at it for twenty minutes, his breath came in rough gasps, and sweat pooled between his shoulder blades.

"Keep going girl," he gasped between breaths. Tasha gave him a look that said she wasn't the one struggling to breathe.

*I could use some help here, Lord.* Maybe God would see fit to give him a burst of super speed or something.

He squinted toward the next curve in the road as a car rounded it. As the vehicle drew closer, Joseph made out the police lights on top.

He gave a gasping laugh-groan. "Not exactly what I had in mind." He wasn't one hundred percent ready to deal with his brother yet, but it was either that or keep running.

He pulled Tasha to a halt, then waved his arms over his head.

The police cruiser slowed and pulled to the side of the road. The passenger window slid down.

"What are you doing running out here?" Zeb looked at him like he'd lost his mind. "Where'd you even come from?"

"My car." Joseph fought to catch his breath, pointing toward where he and Tasha had abandoned the car. "It quit on me a few miles that way. I think it's the alternator."

"Could have told you that thing was on its last legs." Zeb gave his best superior older-brother look. "Why didn't you call?"

Joseph slapped his forehead. "Hey, why didn't I think of that?"

Zeb locked the door. "If you don't want a ride . . ." He inched the car forward.

"Okay, okay." Joseph grabbed at the open window. "Sorry. I didn't have any reception."

"Well, get in." Zeb gestured impatiently at the door as he unlocked it. "Put the dog in the back."

Joseph did as ordered. "Can I use your phone? I'm late for something."

Zeb eyed him. "A date?"

"Maybe. Phone please?" Joseph held out his hand. It wasn't any of Zeb's business.

"How far up the road were you?"

"I don't know. Feels like we ran ten miles." Joseph waved his hand in front of Zeb, still waiting for the phone.

"It's not like I have a magic phone just because I'm a cop." Zeb pulled onto the road. "That's why I have one of these." He picked up his radio and lifted it to his mouth. "I need a tow truck out on Highway Nineteen. Near Sandy Creek Road." He waited for confirmation from dispatch, then glanced at Joseph. "I assume you were headed to Ava's?"

Joseph tensed. Here came the lecture again. "So what if I was?"

Zeb sighed. "So nothing. I wasn't trying to say anything bad about her yesterday. I just wanted you to realize that people change. Feelings change."

Joseph shook his head. That was where Zeb was wrong. "I love her Zeb. Nothing has changed."

Zeb glanced at him out of the corner of his eye but fell silent.

Joseph pointed out the window as they approached the spot where his car had died. “It’s right here.”

Zeb nodded but didn’t slow.

Joseph turned to him and raised an eyebrow. Was his brother really going to sabotage his date?

Zeb shrugged. “It’ll take a while for the tow truck to get here. I’ll take care of it. After I drop you off at Ava’s.”

# Chapter 10

Ava checked the time. Again.

“I don’t know, boy,” she murmured, stroking Griffin’s ears as they sat on the front porch, both watching the driveway. The afternoon sun beat down on her long-sleeved shirt and leggings. She’d briefly considered wearing shorts and a t-shirt, but she wasn’t ready to let Joseph see the full extent of her scars yet.

Ever.

It was the same reason she’d put on makeup even though they’d only be in the woods.

But none of that mattered if Joseph didn’t show up.

He was supposed to have been there forty-five minutes ago. He had always been the most punctual person she knew. If he was late, it meant something was wrong. Maybe he’d had car trouble. Or maybe there was an emergency at the vet.

But she didn’t understand why he hadn’t called.

*Maybe he’s not coming.*

The door opened behind her, but Ava didn’t turn her head. Aunt Lori had already checked on her three times. The first time, Lori had said she was sure Joseph was running behind. The second time, that he was awfully rude not to call when he was so late. And the third time, she hadn’t said anything at all. Just sighed and went back inside.

“Why don’t you come in?” Lori asked now, the gentleness in her voice giving away the words she didn’t say: *He’s not coming.*

"I'm good." Ava kept petting Griffin's ears, and the dog nuzzled closer to her. Sometimes she wondered if she'd trained him as a therapy dog to help others—or to help herself.

Both, she supposed.

"Michael and I were about to play a game of Scrabble. You know you'll kick our butts."

Ava shook her head. The thought of playing Scrabble with her aunt and former teacher was a little too bizarre.

Lori sighed. "Ava, I know Joseph reminds you of how things used to be. But just because he's back doesn't mean you have to give him another chance. He doesn't—"

"It's only a hike," Ava interrupted. She didn't need to have this conversation. She already knew only too well that there was no going back to how things used to be. "It's not a date."

*It's not a date,* she repeated to herself.

Lori sat down beside her on the step. "Maybe it's not a date in your head. But make sure your heart knows that too."

"It does." She had her heart well under lock and key.

Which did not keep it from giving a baby skip at the sound of tires turning onto the gravel at the bottom of the long driveway. The entrance was hidden behind a tunnel of trees, but Ava pushed to her feet, giving Lori a told-you-so look.

"I just don't want you to get hurt," Lori murmured, standing and moving toward the door. "Not again." She retreated into the house, leaving Ava wondering if she should finally set Lori straight about what had happened between her and Joseph—that it had been her, not him, who had called things off.

Not that it mattered, since it wasn't like they were going to call things back on.

Still, maybe it wasn't fair to Joseph to let Lori keep holding this against him.

Well, there'd be time for that later. For now, she watched the driveway, spotting the police cruiser the moment it emerged from the trees. Her heart clenched for a second, then relaxed. Joseph was in the passenger seat, his brother Zeb driving.

Joseph said something to Zeb, then jumped out of the car and opened the back door to let Tasha spring out. The dog bolted straight for Griffin, who was on his feet, sniffing her, in seconds.

Joseph jogged toward Ava as Zeb turned the police car around and pulled away.

"That's one way to make an entrance." Ava couldn't help grinning at him. He hadn't ditched her.

"I'm so sorry." Joseph stopped a few feet in front of her. "My car broke down around Sandy Creek Road. I tried to call, but I didn't have any reception. I was running back to town when Zeb came along."

Ava stared at him. "You were going to run all the way back to town?"

He nodded with a laugh. "I was going to try. Not sure I would have made it. Sorry if I stink before we even start hiking."

Ava laughed and leaned closer, sniffing. He smelled like the same minty lemongrass scent that had always made her feel at home when he was near.

"Nope." She took a few stumbling steps backward, grabbing her water bottle and camera bag off the steps. "Not too stinky."

"Gee, thanks." But Joseph grinned at her. "I don't suppose you'd mind if we take your car?"

"Sure. I'll go get my keys." Ava ducked into the house, popping into the family room to let Aunt Lori know she was leaving. But as she entered the room, it took her a moment to find her voice. Aunt Lori and Mr. Germain were sitting—no, make that *snuggling*—on the couch.

She cleared her throat, and Lori and Mr. Germain both looked over.

"Hey, Ava." Mr. Germain gave her an easy smile. "Want to join us? I need help keeping Lori honest. She seems to think the letters a-i make a word."

"They do." Lori snuggled closer to Mr. Germain. "An ai is a three-toed sloth. You're just jealous of my superior vocabulary."

"I guess so." Mr. Germain dropped a kiss on Lori's forehead.

Ava stared for a moment, then remembered her mission. "I'm heading out." She held up her keys. "Joseph's car broke down."

She gave Lori a pointed look, and her aunt grimaced. "Just be careful, Ava."

"Yep. No bears today."

"Have fun, Ava. Say hi to Joseph for me." Mr. Germain waved cheerfully.

"I will." Ava backed away, then hurried out of the house. She was still shaking her head at the sight of her aunt cuddled up with Mr. Germain. Lori had looked so . . . content.

Had Ava been keeping her aunt from happiness all these years?

"Everything okay?" Joseph asked, tossing a stick that both Griffin and Tasha chased after. "You look . . . perplexed."

Ava laughed as Griffin got to the stick first but left it for Tasha to pick up. "That's a good word for it. Remember Mr. Germain?"

"The history teacher? What about him? Please tell me you weren't one of the girls who had a crush on him."

Ava shook her head. "No. I had—" She bit down hard on her cheek before she could say *you*. "But apparently Aunt Lori was. Or is."

Joseph tilted his head, clearly not following. "Is what?"

"One of the girls with a crush on Mr. Germain. They're in there snuggling right now. He says hi, by the way." She jerked her head toward the house.

"No kidding? That has to be kind of weird."

"Ha. Kind of. I'm glad for her though. She seems really happy." A pang went through her as she remembered how she and Joseph used to be that happy.

Time to focus on something else. "So, since I'm driving, does that mean I get to choose where we go?"

"Sounds fair to me." Joseph loaded the dogs into the backseat of the SUV, then opened Ava's door for her.

"Thank you." She was careful not to meet his eyes as she slid past him into her seat, tucking her camera bag onto the floor behind her. She started the vehicle as she waited for him to climb in the other side. As she pulled onto the road, she risked a look at him. He was watching out the window, looking completely at ease, his lips sporting a small, relaxed smile. Obviously he wasn't fighting the same memories she was. Memories of the way they used to fill the car with constant chatter, mostly about their plans for the future.

Sometimes she wished they'd spent more time focusing on the present, on what they'd had right then—which had been pretty amazing.

"Penny for your thoughts." Joseph interrupted her memories.

"Oh." Her face warmed, and she only hoped she was wearing enough makeup that the pink wouldn't show through. "I was just thinking about . . . Griffin."

*Oh my stars.* Had she said she'd been thinking about her *dog*? But Joseph laughed as Griffin, hearing his name, shoved his face forward so that his muzzle was between them.

"You excited about our hike, boy?" Joseph rubbed at the dog's nose. "No bears this time though, huh?"

They fell silent again, although Ava was sure she could feel Joseph's eyes on her from time to time. She concentrated hard on not looking his way.

But when she finally turned down the road that led to the trail, Joseph made a surprised noise, drawing her eyes to him in spite of her best efforts. "What?"

"Nothing. I just haven't been here in a long time. Not since . . ."

Her breath caught as she realized. This was the first place they'd kissed.

They'd come here for a science project junior year—Mr. Smith had wanted them to collect soil samples for something or other.

Joseph and Ava had paired up and somehow found themselves separated from the rest of the class—Ava had wondered afterward whether Joseph had worked that out on purpose.

She'd just finished scooping some soil into a test tube, and when she'd turned to give it to Joseph, he'd been looking at her in a totally strange way.

He'd lifted his hand and rubbed his fingers lightly over her cheek.

All she could do was stare at him and swallow. They'd been friends since she could remember. But he'd never once touched her face like that.

"Sorry," Joseph had whispered. "You had some dirt." But he hadn't lowered his hand.

"Okay." Her voice had been just as soft, though she didn't know why.

Mr. Smith had called for them then, and Joseph had leaned forward and touched his lips to hers, just for a second—but that second had been long enough to change their lives. Afterwards, he'd grinned at her and dropped his hand from her face, slipping it instead into her hand.

And she'd laced her fingers through his, as if that's where they'd always belonged, and they'd rejoined their class.

Strangely, no one had seemed surprised to see their hands locked. Probably because people had been asking for years if they were a couple.

And right then, Ava had known: their relationship had always been headed for this moment.

She shook herself out of the memory as she pulled the vehicle into a parking spot at the trailhead. "It's easy terrain for Griffin's first time out." She jumped out of the SUV, suddenly needing some air—and some space. A reminder that her past with Joseph was no longer her future.

She opened the back door, and both dogs shot out.

"Wow." Joseph came around the vehicle. "It looks exactly the same."

Ava shrugged. The scenery may be the same—but *they* weren't. She had to remember that.

She grabbed her camera bag out of the vehicle.

"My pack!" Joseph groaned. "It's still in my car."

"Don't worry." Ava patted her bulging bag. "I come prepared."

"I made a picnic." Joseph looked so defeated that Ava had to laugh.

He gave her a mock frown. "I'm glad my incompetence amuses you."

"Always has," she teased.

His eyes widened, but he laughed, and Ava tried hard not to enjoy the sound.

"Come on." She pulled her camera out of her pack and attached it to the strap around her neck. "I want to get some good shots for the gallery."

"Henderson's? You sell there?" Joseph looked impressed, and in spite of herself, Ava was pleased. She'd worked hard to become good enough to sell at the prestigious gallery downtown.

They set off down the trail, which was thankfully wide enough to allow for plenty of distance between them. Ava stopped every now and then to snap pictures of the trees, the occasional wildflower, and the dogs romping through the underbrush. She was sorely tempted to take a picture of Joseph more than once, but she resisted. What would she do with that?

As they walked, Joseph asked her questions about her photography, and she asked about his veterinary practice. Both of them steered very decidedly away from any topics that related to their past.

To her surprise, Ava found herself enjoying the conversation. The only person she talked to most days was Aunt Lori—unless you counted Griffin. It was nice to talk to someone who didn't already know everything that went on in her life—what little there was to tell.

"Wow." Joseph stopped as they came to a spot on the trail that opened up to a spectacular view of the river below. "I missed this."

"Me too." The words were out before Ava realized that he could have meant the view—or being with her. "I mean, I haven't been here in a long time either."

Joseph's smile wrapped her up tighter than a hug, and she started walking again, picking up the pace. "So, you were saying that you're hoping to modernize the office?" she asked as Joseph caught up to her.

"Um. Yeah." He sounded slightly confused, and Ava realized they'd had that conversation a good ten minutes ago. But she'd needed something, anything, to chase away the memories that had almost caught up with her back there.

"I don't think Dr. Gallagher ever threw a single piece of paper away. There are records in there from before we were born. Probably from before my dad was born." Joseph chuckled. "I want to switch everything over to digital."

"That makes sense." What didn't make sense was the disappointment that flooded her as she spotted the trailhead and her car. Had they really reached the end of the loop already?

She ignored the feeling. It was obviously better if she spent less time with Joseph, rather than more. Otherwise, she might start to want things she knew she could never have.

She pulled the camera strap off her neck and opened the vehicle, tucking her equipment back into her case. "See. No bears."

"All right. You win. No bears. But it wasn't *so* bad to hike with Tasha and me, was it?" Joseph came up next to her and nudged her arm. He'd done it a thousand times before, and yet this time—this time it made her want to slide closer to him. She closed her pack and stepped away, calling to the dogs to get in.

"You're right. Tasha was a lot of fun," she answered as she shut the door behind the dogs. "She'll have to come with me and Griffin next time too."

"Sorry." Joseph opened the driver's door for her. "We're a package deal. You want the dog, you have to put up with me too."

"Hmm." Ava stepped past him, accidentally catching a hint of lemongrass again. "I'll have to think about that. You're a lot to put up with, you know."

"I know." Joseph grinned and closed her door.

Ava let out a quick breath, fighting to get her own grin under wraps as Joseph got in the car too.

But he turned uncharacteristically serious eyes on her as she pulled onto the road. "Can I ask you something?"

Ava's stomach plummeted. They'd managed to keep things light and breezy so far today. To ignore the past, even if it had been hovering between every word.

Why couldn't it stay that way?

She waited silently, knowing he'd ask whether she invited him to or not.

"Are you hungry?" His voice was flat, completely serious, and she let out a relieved laugh.

And then realized she had to answer his question.

The truth was, she was starved. But—

"This was only supposed to be a hike, Joseph. Not dinner."

"I know. But I spent all that time packing a picnic we didn't get to eat . . ."

He turned toward her, and she made the mistake of glancing at those blue eyes.

He must have read in her expression that he'd won because he smiled. "Murf's?"

She chewed her lip. Murf's had been their favorite hangout in high school, and plenty of high school kids still frequented the place. It was the kind of place she avoided like a rattlesnake these days.

"We can get it to go," he said. "Eat it at my house. Maybe you could give Tasha her first lesson."

She glanced at him again. This time his eyes were understanding. He was giving her an out, so she didn't have to be seen in public. Or maybe so he didn't have to be seen in public with her.

Either way, she couldn't deny that Murf's sounded amazing. And if she went home, she'd likely be grilled by Aunt Lori—or have to spend the evening watching her aunt and Mr. Germain cuddle.

"Can we get a shake?" She stopped herself, flustered. They'd always shared a shake when they went to Murf's. "I mean, can we each get a shake?"

Joseph grinned at her. "Obviously."

"All right then." Ava pointed her car toward River Falls. "Let's do it."

# Chapter 11

So far, today had gone even better than he'd hoped.

Joseph stood in line at Murf's and glanced out the window toward where Ava remained in the vehicle with the dogs.

Any doubts he may have had about whether she would still be the same person, whether they would still be good together, had been erased today.

Ava was quieter now, more reserved maybe, but there was also a new air of thoughtfulness about her. And her laugh was as contagious as ever—even if she didn't unleash it as often as she used to.

He stepped to the counter and placed his order, smiling as he requested two shakes. If things kept going this well, it wouldn't be long before they shared one shake—and one straw—again.

The order was ready quickly, and he thanked the server, then hurried to the door, nearly running over a woman on her way in.

"Sorry." He bit back a groan when he realized it was Madison, the awkward encounter in the grocery store still fresh in his mind.

"Two shakes." Madison raised a thin eyebrow. "So you really are seeing someone." She offered a laugh that sounded forced. "I have to admit, I was getting a little paranoid that you were blowing me off the other day."

"Of course not," Joseph mumbled.

"So who's the lucky lady?" Madison glanced over her shoulder toward the parking lot, her gaze stopping directly on Ava's SUV. "Ah, I should have known y'all would be back together."

"Well—" He didn't know how to say he was still working on that part.

"I want to say hi. I never see her around."

Joseph had a feeling that was the way Ava liked it. But Madison was already on her way to the vehicle.

He jogged to catch up, careful not to jostle the shakes.

Ava's eyes widened as she spotted them, and Joseph made an apologetic face that he wasn't sure she interpreted correctly.

He climbed into the passenger seat, fending off the dogs, as Madison rounded the vehicle to stand at Ava's open window.

"Hey there, Ava. I haven't seen you in ages." Madison's voice was sweet enough, and Joseph let out a pent-up breath.

"Hi, Madison." Ava, too, sounded friendly enough.

This was going to be fine.

"Where do you keep yourself hidden these days? Locked away in a tower?" Madison giggled at her own joke.

"Nope. In my cabin in the woods." Ava's response was cool and calm.

"Guess you were waiting for your Prince Charming to come let you out." Madison looked past Ava and winked at Joseph. "I knew when he left me at prom that he wasn't over you."

Joseph blinked slowly, averting his gaze so he wouldn't have to see Ava's reaction to that. He was sure Ava already knew he'd gone to prom with Madison—things like that didn't stay quiet in a town like River Falls—but that didn't mean he wanted to remind her of it. Especially not now, when things were going so well.

"Anyway—" Madison took a step backward. "I've gotta run. I'm meeting friends." She fluttered her fingers in a wave, then turned and flounced toward the restaurant.

Joseph let out a breath and glanced at Ava. Once upon a time, they would have laughed together over something like this. But Ava was watching Madison as she joined up with a group of women he recognized from high school.

Ava looked . . . wistful? Envious?

"Let's go. Before our food gets cold and our shakes get warm." Joseph adjusted the food on his lap so it wouldn't spill.

But Ava's hands didn't move toward the keys. She was still gazing at the blue awning over the entrance to Murf's, though Madison and her friends had disappeared inside.

"Ava?"

"Hmm? Oh." She grabbed at the keys and turned on the engine. As she pulled out of the parking lot, Joseph gave her directions to his house.

She didn't say a word the entire drive, and by the time they got there, he was next to certain she was going to dump him at the curb and screech away the moment he got out of the vehicle.

But she shut off the engine, then unbuckled her seatbelt and opened her door.

He took a deep breath, telling himself this was it.

This was the opportunity he'd been waiting for.

So he'd better not blow it.

# Chapter 12

She shouldn't be here.

Ava let her eyes rove Joseph's living room again as she waited for him to come back from cleaning up the "dishes" from their dinner.

His home was warm and cozy—and just as organized as she'd known it would be.

And the longer she was here, the more she liked being here.

The more she liked being with *him*.

Which was dangerous.

Her eyes fell on a clay pot that had very obviously been broken and then glued back together. She got up and moved toward it. Behind her, she heard Joseph come into the room.

"You still have this?" She picked it up and turned it over in her hands. She'd made it in vacation Bible school the summer after sixth grade, and it had been nearly flawless. The teacher had praised her for the extra details she'd added—etched flowers and pomegranates—and shown it to the class.

But just as Ava had picked it up to put it in a safe spot, Joseph had crashed into her, and the pot had tumbled to the floor, splintering into half a dozen pieces.

"Remember how mad you were?" From the distance of his voice, she could tell he was still on the other side of the room.

"I remember." Ava laughed at the younger her, who had been so broken up about a hunk of clay. "I accused you of destroying my masterpiece."

"Yeah, and you wouldn't take it back after I glued it. But I couldn't just throw your masterpiece away."

"Even though it's hideous?" Ava ran her finger over an imperfectly aligned seam.

"Hey, I think I did a pretty good job putting it back together." Joseph's voice softened. "Anyway, just because something's broken doesn't mean it's not beautiful."

Ava's breath hitched at the significance she thought she detected in his words. But she refused to look at him to see if what she thought she heard—what she wanted to hear, perhaps—was correct.

She set the pot back on the shelf, her fingers going to the rough skin of her face by habit. Madison's flawless complexion popped into her head—her flawless complexion and her giggling voice as she'd talked about going to prom with Joseph.

What was Ava doing here, letting herself pretend nothing had changed? "I should go."

Joseph made a sound of dissent. "What about Tasha's lesson? You can't break your promise to her."

Ava sighed, looking toward where Tasha and Griffin were curled up together on the floor.

Tasha looked up, giving her the same puppy dog plea Griffin was so good at.

Did Ava really feel compelled to keep a promise she'd made to a dog?

"Fine. Just for a few minutes."

But an hour later, long shadows traced across the grass as the sun hovered at the edge of the ridge to the west. And she was still there, still working with the dog, still enjoying every moment with Joseph.

That was it. She had to go before she wanted more.

She patted Tasha's head. "Good girl. Honestly, I don't think you'll need much more training."

"But you'll still help, right?" Joseph's look was hopeful and eager.

Ava bit her lip. This could be dangerous. "I'll try," she finally settled on. "If I have time." He didn't need to know that she had nothing but time most days.

She shuffled awkwardly, not quite sure how to say goodbye to him. She wasn't going to pat his head like she did Tasha's, obviously. But a hug seemed like too much—even if every time she looked at him she remembered the feel of his arms around her.

She slid her hands into her back pockets, staring toward the pink flowers of his neighbor's crape myrtle tree. "Keep working on 'leave it' with her. I'll set up the test for a couple of weeks from now. She should be ready."

Joseph laughed. "I appreciate your optimism. Maybe we can—"

Ava couldn't let him finish that sentence. "Thanks for the hike. And for dinner. It was nice." Okay, it was the best day she'd had since . . . since the last time she'd spent the day with Joseph. But that had been a long time ago. And this had been a one-time thing.

"It *was* nice, wasn't it?" Joseph's eyes grabbed hers, and his smile put a tiny chink in the safe around her heart.

"Griffin, let's go." She tore her eyes away from Joseph and clapped for the dog to get up from the spot where he'd been rolling in the grass.

"Ava, wait." Joseph's voice was soft but urgent, and Ava's heart tried to bang another dent into the safe.

She let her eyes come back to his but made herself look away quickly. Whatever he was going to say, she wouldn't be able to resist it if she was drawn into them.

Joseph cleared his throat. "I just wondered if I'll see you at church tomorrow?"

"Oh." Ava licked her dry lips. "Probably not." She tried to sound nonchalant, even as guilt pressed at her.

"You don't go to church anymore?"

"Not really. No." The thought of stepping through those doors and sitting among all those people—she fought off the shudder.

"Why not?" Joseph moved to the porch and lowered himself onto the top step, pointing to the spot next to him.

Ava remained on her feet. "It's complicated."

"I just spent eight years studying to be a vet. I'm good at complicated." Joseph's smile was warm, inviting, free of judgment.

Ava sighed, running a hand over her cheek. "Since the—" She choked on the sentence. They'd never talked about that night before. But she made herself go on. "Since the fire, I've developed some agoraphobia."

"Bless you," Joseph said, as if she'd sneezed, giving her a blank look.

"I thought you were good at complicated," she teased, moving to lean against the porch railing. Griffin looked from her to Joseph, then settled at Joseph's feet. "Basically, the first time I tried to go back to church—it was maybe six months or so after the fire—I had a panic attack. Right there in the middle of church. I kept thinking of all those people looking at me, and suddenly I couldn't breathe. I mean, not like I *thought* I couldn't breathe. I literally couldn't catch my breath. Like someone was squeezing a vice around my lungs." Even talking about it now made her gasp for breath. "My heart was pounding so hard I couldn't hear the music, and I was shaking. And all I could think was that I was going to die right there in the middle of church, with all those people looking at me."

"What happened?" Joseph's voice was soft, comforting, as it wrapped around her.

She shrugged. "I wanted to get up and leave, but I couldn't get my limbs to work. So I just sat there. It passed after fifteen minutes or so.

But I could barely walk out of there at the end of the service, my legs were wobbling so badly."

"Have you ever had more attacks?"

"Yeah. It's why I don't go many places. Just home and to my studio. Some days that's hard too, but it helps that there are never a lot of people there at once." She broke off, realizing that there was now one other place she'd gone—here. Where she felt oddly safe.

"So you don't go places because you're afraid of having another attack?"

Ava nodded. "And *that* is the definition of agoraphobia. Avoiding places or situations out of fear you'll have a panic attack."

"Is there anything that can help?" Joseph slid a few inches closer to her, and Ava crossed her arms to fend off the desire to let him wrap her up and keep her safe. That wasn't his job anymore.

"I was seeing a counselor for a while. She suggested I take someone with me when I go somewhere I'm worried about. But Lori is busy. And you know how she feels about church." When she was younger, Ava had pushed for Lori to come with her—but Lori would only drop Ava off at the door and pick her up afterward. It was how Ava had ended up spending most Sundays sitting with Joseph and his family.

"Anyway—" Ava brushed at invisible dirt on her sleeve. "Your daddy comes to see me sometimes." Though the last several times Pastor Calvano had called, she'd put him off. Come to think of it, it had probably been three years or more since the last time she'd met with him.

Joseph touched her elbow. "If you ever need someone to go with you, you know I'm here. Okay?"

Ava swallowed and nodded, taking a step away from the porch. She didn't want to leave. But she *did* want to put some space between them.

A warm hand grabbed hers and pulled her toward him. The moment she turned to look at him, she knew she shouldn't have.

Joseph chose to ignore Ava's quick head shake. He'd already waited far too long to do this.

He stood and grabbed her other hand too, mostly because she looked poised to run away.

"Ava, I miss you. I've missed you every day for the past eight years."

Ava shook her head again, harder this time, the last rays of the sinking sun setting the red strands of her hair alight.

She pulled her hands out of his and took a step backwards. "Joseph, please don't."

"Don't what?" He followed her as she fled toward her vehicle. "Don't tell you that there hasn't been a day that's gone by that I haven't thought of you? Don't tell you that if I could go back and do it over again, I—"

"I said don't!" She whirled on him, her voice fierce, the green of her eyes glistening.

The plea that was on his lips fell away. He couldn't keep himself from reaching for her hands again, but she swung them out of his grasp.

"Why?" It didn't make sense. They were still perfect together. She had to see that.

"I just can't." Her whisper was filled with a desperation Joseph had never heard from her before. "Promise you won't ask me for more than friendship. That you won't ask me out. Ever."

The kick of her words hit Joseph in the gut. This was the same woman he'd once promised forever. Now she wanted him to promise the opposite? "You really want me to promise that?"

She nodded.

Joseph blew out a long breath, turning his head to watch the sun slip below the mountains to the west. If this was what she wanted, he didn't have a right to deny it. No matter how much it hurt him. "I promise." He could only manage a whisper.

"Thank you." Her smile was wobbly. "We *can* still be friends though, right?"

"Always." Joseph stepped forward and pulled her into a quick, friendly hug, complete with back slap. "See?"

"Good." Ava ducked out of his arms and called for Griffin.

A second later, she backed out of the driveway with a small, sad wave.

Or maybe it only looked sad because his own heart was shattered. After eight years of waiting, this was how things were going to end?

Maybe he should have pleaded with her, tried to convince her she was wrong. But he knew Ava. Once she'd made up her mind about something, it was nearly impossible to change it. At least without help.

He shook his head letting a small grin cheer him. "I promised not to ask her out," he said to Tasha. "I didn't promise I wouldn't pray she'd change her mind."

# Chapter 13

"Do you not like Michael?" Aunt Lori barged into the kitchen Friday morning, and Ava jumped, looking up from the Bible she'd been reading. She'd dug it out of her desk this morning, though she still wasn't sure why, only that ever since Joseph had asked her about church, she'd been thinking more and more about how she'd let her attention to her faith fade over the last few years—since the fire, if she was being honest.

"What?" Ava closed the Bible. She'd spent the past ten minutes staring at Jeremiah 29:11, once her favorite verse: "'For I know the plans I have for you,' declares the Lord, 'plans to prosper you and not to harm you, plans to give you hope and a future.'" Believing that had been easy once, when she could see her whole life mapped out before her, stretching out forever. But now—now her forever had shattered into more pieces than that old clay pot Joseph had held onto. And unlike the pot, it was impossible to put it back together again.

She forced her attention back to Lori. "Why would you ask that?"

"Well, you hardly said a word to him at dinner last night. You didn't laugh at his cowboy joke. And he said you change the subject whenever he mentions helping with the yearbook." Lori folded her arms. "Is this too weird for you? Me dating one of your old teachers?"

"What? No. I mean, well, yes. It's weird."

Lori made a sound like she was about to speak, but Ava kept going. "It's weird. But not bad. You seem happy."

"I am." Lori grinned like a lovesick teenager. "But what's going on with you? You haven't been yourself all week. Since you went hiking with Joseph." Lori raised an eyebrow. "I think I told you it was a bad idea."

Ava sighed. She hadn't heard a word from Joseph all week—not even a text. And her constant obsession with checking for one was only proof she'd made the right decision when she'd made him promise not to ask her for more than friendship.

Because no matter how much she wanted to be with him again, she was his past. Not his future. And the sooner they both accepted that, the better.

Still, she'd thought that remaining friends meant . . . well, that they'd talk at least.

*You could text him, you know.*

"He doesn't deserve you, Ava, you know that, right? Not after the way he walked away—"

"I made him." The confession shot off her tongue. It wasn't fair to Joseph to let Aunt Lori think he was that kind of guy.

Lori stared at her. "What do you mean, you made him? You made him what?"

"Walk away." Ava swallowed. "I told him I didn't want to see him again after the fire. I broke up with him, not the other way around."

Lori stared, as if she didn't believe Ava. "He must have done something to make you—"

Ava shook her head, blinking hard so she wouldn't give in to the burning at the back of her eyes. "He didn't do anything, Aunt Lori. He was just himself. The same perfect Joseph as always."

"Well." Aunt Lori blew out a breath and leaned against the counter. "Why did you do that?"

"Because he deserved better," Ava whispered. "He had this whole big future in front of him, and I had this . . ." She waved a hand around the room. "This small life."

"No offense taken." Lori laughed but then made her way across the room and pulled Ava into a quick hug. "Your life is not small. And there is no one better, you got that? If Joseph's not smart enough to figure that out, he's not worth it. Right?"

Ava nodded once. There was no need to tell Aunt Lori that Joseph wanted to ask her out again. Now that she knew the truth about their breakup, Ava couldn't guarantee her aunt wouldn't side with Joseph. And she couldn't risk having two people trying to convince her to date him. She wasn't sure she'd be strong enough to resist that.

And she had to resist it—at all costs. Because as much as Joseph might *think* he still wanted to be with her, sooner or later he would realize she wasn't the kind of woman he should be with. That he could do so much better. That he deserved someone whole and unbroken—someone like Madison.

Because he *would* realize it eventually, that much she was certain of. And she was pretty sure she wasn't strong enough to handle it when he did.

Anyway, he may have looked hurt for a second when she'd made him promise not to ask her for a relationship—but he hadn't argued. He'd made the promise without a fight.

Which only went to show—his heart wasn't at stake the way hers was.

Joseph drummed his fingers on his car's steering wheel as he pulled out of his driveway. After a week without a vehicle, it was good to have the car back.

If only it were as easy to get back into Ava's life.

He'd left her alone all week, trying to show her that he was respecting her wishes. But it had taken every last ounce of his willpower, and he wasn't sure how much longer he could go without at least texting her. If he was being honest, he'd hoped that she'd realize she missed him and maybe stop by with Griffin or give him a call or even a teeny-tiny text. But he'd gotten nothing but radio silence from her since last Saturday.

Maybe he was crazy to hold out any hope at all. But after waiting eight years, he wasn't going to give up over a couple of days of silence. In fact, as soon as he got to work, he'd text her. She'd said they could still be friends. And friends texted each other, right? Nothing more natural in the world.

Now he just had to figure out *what* to text her.

As he pulled into the driveway of River Falls Veterinary, he was still trying to come up with something. "How are you doing?" seemed too open-ended. "What are you doing?" was too intrusive. "Thinking of you" would only make her put up more walls.

He sighed, patting Tasha's head as he parked in the farthest spot from the door, leaving the closer spots for his clients. He'd been swamped all week, and the small parking lot tended to fill up fast. "This is harder than you'd think."

Tasha gave him a sniff, and Joseph laughed. "If only it were that easy."

He got out of the car and opened Tasha's door. The moment she was outside, she lifted her nose to the air and sniffed for a second, then bolted toward the front door.

"Tasha, wait." Fortunately, there was no one else in the parking lot this early in the morning. "Tasha, come."

But the dog ignored him, charging straight for a large box that was blocking the front door. Joseph frowned at it. He didn't remember ordering anything.

Tasha scratched at the box, whining.

Joseph tilted his head, watching her. "What is it, girl?" He lengthened his stride.

When he was a dozen yards away, he heard it.

Little yips.

He jogged the last few steps and pulled the top of the box open.

Tasha jostled him out of the way as she vaulted onto her hind legs, her front paws perched on the edge of the box, her nose poking into it.

Joseph nudged her aside so he could see.

"Holy smokes." He reached into the box and plucked out a wriggling puppy—white and brown speckled and no more than six weeks old, by the looks of it. Inside the box, another eight pups barked up at him.

He looked from the puppies to Tasha to the sky and chuckled. "You're a genius, Lord."

He knew exactly what to do next.

# Chapter 14

"You know what, boy?" Ava snapped her fingers to call Griffin. Aunt Lori had left half an hour ago, and Ava had been sitting here pining for Joseph long enough. "Let's go for a hike."

Griffin shot to his feet, his tail swinging from side to side. But his eyes questioned. *Was this a good idea?*

Ava ignored his look. It wasn't like she'd promised Joseph she'd *never* hike without him. Just that one time. And besides, it wasn't like he was offering to go with her again.

She slipped on her boots, grabbed her camera bag, and led Griffin toward the back door.

She was just pulling it open when her phone rang. She groaned and considered ignoring it, but she was waiting to hear from a potential new client to schedule a portrait session.

She pulled the phone out of her pocket, glancing at the screen.

A disbelieving breath escaped her, and she let her finger hover over the screen. Should she answer it?

She wanted to hear his voice so badly. She moved her finger toward the *answer* icon.

But hearing his voice would only confuse her more. She needed to decline the call.

Before she could, Griffin rammed his head against her leg, making her nearly drop the phone. As she snatched it from the air, she heard a voice calling, "Hello? Ava?"

"Are you kidding me?" she hissed at Griffin, who looked up at her with his big, innocent eyes.

She must have bumped *answer* when she'd caught the phone. Now she had two options: put it to her ear and say hello like a human being—or hang up on Joseph.

Her finger moved toward the *end call* button. But she wasn't strong enough to do it.

Growling at herself, she lifted the phone to her ear. "Hey." She was proud of the way she managed to keep the delighted anticipation burning in her chest out of her voice.

"Hey. What are you up to right now?"

Ava looked at the leash in her hand and the dog watching her expectantly. "Um. Nothing. Why?"

"You were about to go for a hike, weren't you?"

Ava spluttered. Did the man have security cameras on her? "How could you possibly know that?"

"Griffin needs a quieter tag." She could hear Joseph's suppressed laugh through the phone. "Thought you could get away with it, huh?"

"Well, that's— I'm not—" She gave up. "I never promised we wouldn't ever hike again without you. We can't sit around here and wait for you to be available, you know."

"You didn't ask if I was available," Joseph pointed out.

"I— That's—" Ava spluttered. There had to be a better comeback than that. "Well, are you?" Defiance made her words sharp. She hoped he'd say no. Prove her point.

"Actually no, not at the moment," Joseph answered, and Ava told herself she felt vindicated.

"Are you?" he added.

"Am I what?"

"Available?" He sounded amused.

"Joseph, we already talked about—"

"Just trust me. Oops—where you going there, little guy?" There was shuffling in the background.

"What? Joseph, what's going on there? Who are you talking to?"

"Just get down to my office as fast as you can. You're going to want to see this. And bring your camera."

He clicked off the line, and Ava pulled the phone away from her ear.

"That was odd, right?" she asked Griffin.

The dog wagged his tail at her, his tongue lolling out the side of his mouth.

She tucked her phone away and stared at the leash still in her hand. They should go for their planned hike. It didn't matter what was going on down at Joseph's office. Didn't matter that he had asked her to come. Didn't matter, even, that his voice had been as warm and comfortable as ever.

She chewed her lip, telling herself not to give in to the curiosity.

She did battle for five minutes before giving up and grabbing her car keys and camera bag. She'd bring Griffin with her for backup. Not that he would be much help, since he seemed to have developed a strong preference for Joseph during their one day together.

All the way to River Falls, she told herself this was a bad idea. Still, she kept driving, and thirty minutes later, as she pulled into the parking lot of River Falls Veterinary, a flutter worked through her stomach and up toward her heart. But there was no reason to be nervous. One thing she knew about Joseph—when he made a promise, he kept it. There was no chance he'd renew the question he'd almost asked the other night.

She let out a quick breath, opened her door, and snapped on Griffin's leash. "All right, boy. Let's go see what this is about."

As soon as she opened the door of the veterinary office, she was met by utter chaos. The tiniest puppies she'd ever seen scurried helter skelter across the lobby, yipping and chasing each other.

But the moment they spotted Ava and Griffin, the little critters made a beeline for them.

"Oh my stars. Look at y'all." Gasping and laughing, Ava lowered herself into a crouch to greet them. She scooped up the first one to reach her, then held out a hand to let the others sniff at her fingers. Next to her, Griffin stood stock still, though his tail wagged wildly from side to side, knocking Ava in the back.

"It's okay," she said to him. "They're puppies."

Griffin gave her a questioning look, then lowered his head and began sniffing.

Ava lifted the puppy in her hands to her face and nuzzled its soft fur against her cheek. Its puppy scent—a mix of warmth and kibble—brought back the comforting feeling she'd soaked up from Griffin when he was a pup.

"I see you've met my visitors." Joseph's laughing voice reached her, and she looked up to find him emerging from the hallway with yet another puppy. Tasha trotted at his side, eyeing the critter he carried.

"How many are there?"

"Nine. Left in a box on the doorstep." He set the puppy in his hands down and picked up another.

The puppy he'd just released took a wobbly step. It seemed much less stable on its feet than the others.

"Is she all right?" Ava pushed to her feet and moved closer to the pup.

"One of her back feet is slightly twisted." Joseph rested the pup he'd just picked up on the waiting room counter, probing at it.

"Isn't there anything you can do?" Ava watched as the puppy in front of her tipped over, its legs splayed Bambi-style on the floor.

"It's not severe enough to need surgery. She'll be fine. Eventually, she'll adapt and be running around just like her brothers and sisters."

Ava frowned. How could he be so sure the puppy would adjust? Look how she was already separated from the others, who were all now exploring under the waiting room chairs. Some things a person—or dog—just didn't adjust to.

"What are you going to do with them all?"

Joseph eyed her, a glimmer she recognized only too well in his eyes. "That's where you come in."

"Me?" Ava held up her hands. "Aunt Lori barely let me get *one* dog."

Joseph's laugh scared the puppy in his hands, and he gave it a reassuring pat before setting it on the floor. "Not to adopt them. To take pictures of them, so we can post them online. Find good homes for them."

"What about the shelter in Brampton?"

Joseph shook his head. "They don't have room for this many. So I said I'd take care of them."

Of course he had. Joseph hadn't met a problem yet that he didn't think he could solve.

"So will you help me?" His look was warm and hopeful.

Ava looked away. But it wasn't like she could say no to puppies.

# Chapter 15

Joseph slapped his hands against his cheeks to wake himself up.

It turned out that taking care of nine puppies night and day, on top of seeing his regular clients, was exhausting.

Fortunately, it had only taken six days to find good homes for all but one of them.

"What are we going to do with you?" he asked the puppy with the leg deformity, whom he had nicknamed Princess.

The puppy looked up from Tasha's dog bed, where it had plopped for a nap half an hour ago. From the floor next to the dog bed, Tasha gave him a look that said she was not amused.

Joseph glanced at the time. One o'clock. That meant he had an hour free before his next patient. An hour he should probably spend charting this morning's visits.

He tapped his pen on his desk, his thoughts going to Ava as they inevitably did whenever he had a free moment—or when he didn't.

What he needed was a way to spend time with her that wasn't a date. That way he could keep his promise—but she could also see that she'd been wrong to ask him to make it.

He'd thought the puppies were his answer. But aside from taking pictures of them last week, she hadn't stopped by to visit them once. At least the dogs had given him an excuse to text updates every time one found a home. And Ava had even texted back. But it wasn't enough. He needed to *see* her. To *talk to* her.

He stared vaguely at the family picture on his desk as he considered other excuses to spend time with her.

The idea came on so slowly that it took him a moment to realize his own genius.

But when he did, he picked up his phone and dialed, tapping his fingers impatiently as he waited for his sister to answer.

The moment she did, he launched right into his question. "You guys are coming home for the weekend, right?"

"Hello to you too." Grace sounded exasperated, but he knew it was an act. His sister was always happy to hear from him.

"Yeah, yeah. Hello, Grace. How are things?" He played along.

"Great. We just put in this coffee bar and—"

"Grace." His exasperation wasn't an act.

His sister laughed. "Sorry. But I *am* going to tell you all about the coffee bar when we get there. And just for that, the story is going to be twice as long. But to answer your question, yes, we're coming this weekend. Actually, we have some big news."

"Great. Wait. You do? Are you having a baby?" His sister had only been married to Levi Donovan for a year now. But he supposed that was plenty long enough for them to be expecting.

Grace laughed. "No. Not that kind of news."

"Well, what then? Is Levi coming out of retirement?" The Titans sure could use him on the field again.

"No." Grace laughed again. "We'll tell you this weekend. Now, is there a reason you're so eager to have us home? Or do you just miss your big sister?"

"Oh yeah." How could he have gotten side-tracked? "Benjamin's going to be home from school for the weekend too. So I was thinking we should get some new family pictures taken. Maybe on Saturday?"

Grace was silent. Joseph pulled the phone away from his ear, but they were still connected. "Grace?"

"Sorry. You shocked me speechless. Aren't you the same little boy who hid in the woods for an hour so you wouldn't have to have your picture taken?"

"That was a long time ago." And besides, a bad case of poison ivy had taught him his lesson.

"I've still never seen you willingly be photographed. What gives?"

Joseph ran a hand over his hair, grateful his sister couldn't see the heat rising to his face. "Nothing. I just thought it'd be nice to have some new pictures. You know Mama would have wanted us to. Family picture day was always her favorite. And we haven't done it since she died."

"That's actually a sweet idea," Grace sounded surprised, and a twinge of guilt pinged Joseph. Was he really using their deceased Mama to convince her? Heaven help him.

"Great. I'll call Ava to set it up. I'll see you—"

"Ah, so that's what this is about." Grace's voice took on that annoying, know-it-all tone that was so similar to Zeb's. No wonder those two got along so well.

"What what's all about?" But he knew the innocent act was useless. His sister knew him too well. "Maybe a little," he admitted. "But mostly it's because I think we should do the pictures."

"I'm glad, Joseph. You two were always good together."

"Preaching to the choir. If you wanted to mention that to Ava, though . . ."

Grace laughed. "I'll see if I can work it in."

As soon as he'd hung up, Joseph started to dial again.

But then he had a better idea.

He had a rare lull in his schedule, and he was going to make use of it. He stuck his phone in his pocket and pushed his chair back. "I'm going to go get some pie," he said to Tasha. "Keep an eye on Princess."

Tasha sighed and laid her head on her paws.

Joseph marched out the door and locked it behind him, then set off at a good clip toward the pie shop, squinting against the light bouncing off the river behind the storefronts. Though it was already the beginning of September, the day was hot and sticky, the sun scorching against his hair.

Even so, he kicked up his pace. He'd noticed Ava's car outside her studio this morning, and he didn't want to miss her.

Ava opened her desk drawer and dropped her phone inside.

She'd wasted the past fifteen minutes rereading the texts Joseph had sent this week, trying to convince herself that she did *not* need to see the puppies before the rest of them were adopted out. And more importantly, that she did *not* need to see Joseph.

"You just have to stay busy," she muttered to herself. And she knew exactly where she could start.

She tried to work up the energy to clean as she dragged herself toward the back room of her studio. But all she could do as she stood in the doorway gazing at the mess was groan. Organizing this clutter was going to be a gargantuan task.

"Well, you wanted a distraction," she said out loud. "This should do."

"Do you always talk to yourself?"

She jumped, even though she recognized the voice. "Oh my stars. Joseph." She gave herself a second to put on her neutral, of-course-I'm-not-pleased-to-see-you expression, then turned toward him. "What are you doing here?"

He was wearing a smile and holding pie.

Her two weaknesses.

"You asked for a distraction. So here I am."

Ava tried to resist the urge to smile back but failed.

*Be strong*, she warned herself.

"What are we distracting you from?" Joseph glanced over her shoulder, his eyes widening at the clutter.

"Nothing." She brushed past him toward the front of the building. Not that there was any reason to go up there, but maybe if she got him closer to the door, it would be easier to get him *out* the door. "And I repeat, what are you doing here?"

"Delivering pie." He followed her to her desk, then held out a piece to her.

She closed her eyes. Blueberry. Her favorite. There was no way she could resist.

She took the pie but satisfied her conscience by giving Joseph a disapproving look. "You can't just be dropping by and bringing pie."

Joseph opened the plastic clamshell holding his own slice of lemon meringue. "Sorry. I didn't realize friends couldn't bring friends pie." He picked up the plastic fork from his container and cut off a huge chunk, stuffing the pie in his mouth with a satisfied "mmm."

That was it.

She couldn't help it.

She was weak.

She opened her own clamshell and dug out a big bite, sighing as the sweet-tart flavor of the berries popped against her tongue.

"Still think I shouldn't bring you pie?"

She ignored the question, taking another bite.

"I thought you'd like to know two more puppies got adopted this morning." Joseph spoke between bites.

"That's wonderful. How many does that leave?"

"Only one." Joseph polished off his pie and tossed the container in the trash. "Princess."

The one with the deformed leg. That figured. "Poor little thing."

Joseph shrugged. "I'm sure she'll find a home. Unless you want to take her." It wasn't the first time he'd asked.

"You know Aunt Lori would kill me." She shoveled the last bite of her pie into her mouth. Surely, with the pie gone, Joseph would be on his way too.

But he settled himself against the edge of her desk. "Got a question to ask you."

Ava gave him a warning look, but Joseph pressed on. "Grace and her husband are coming home this weekend, and we were hoping to have some family portraits done . . ."

Ava started to shake her head. If it wasn't a good idea to spend time with Joseph, it wasn't a good idea to spend time with his family either. It'd be too easy to fall back in love with being surrounded by them.

But Joseph's eyes captured hers. "Please, Ava. We haven't done them since Mama . . . We thought it'd be nice to have someone who knew her. Someone who could help us find a way to honor her in the pictures."

Ava sighed. "That was low."

Joseph raised an eyebrow. "Did it work?"

Ava bit her lip. "When do you want to do them?"

# Chapter 16

Ava had barely parked her vehicle in the driveway of Pastor Calvano's house Saturday afternoon when Joseph was pulling her door open. Unable to wait for her to get out, Griffin trampled over her lap and shot out of the vehicle to greet Tasha.

"Thanks for that," she said dryly to Joseph, concentrating on not noticing the way his light blue button down brought out the depths of blue in his eyes—or the way his shoulders filled it out.

"Come on." Joseph's tone was eager. "I have a surprise for you."

"More pie?"

A grin rocketed across Joseph's lips. "Better than pie."

"What's better than pie? Anyway, I thought I was here to take pictures of your family."

"You are. But you have to see this first." He followed as she got out of the car and made her way to the back to unload her equipment. She grabbed her camera bag and was about to sling it over her shoulder when he plucked it from her hands. She gave him a look but let him carry it.

"Now are you ready?" Joseph reached to close the back hatch of the SUV, but she pretended to consider.

"You're ready." He closed the hatch with a slam. "Come on." He reached for her arm but withdrew his hand before making contact.

Ava let out a long breath. "You know I don't like surprises."

"Just trust me. You already love this one." Joseph's eyes were practically dancing, and Ava found that she did trust him.

It was strange how natural it felt to be following him to the door of his father's house. How much time had she spent with his family over the years?

He opened the door, and she checked over her shoulder. Currently, Tasha and Griffin were chasing around the yard, though they clearly didn't know who was chasing whom. "What about the dogs?"

"They'll be fine out here. Come on. She's in the kitchen." Joseph held the door open and gestured her through.

Ah, so the surprise must be his sister. Though Grace was five years older than her, Ava had always looked up to her as a big sister. It'd been far too long since she'd seen her.

Ava walked through the familiar living room toward the kitchen, Joseph following so close behind her that his scent tickled her nose—and made her want to stop and breathe it in all day.

She hurried into the kitchen and circled to the far side of the island to get out of Joseph-scent range. "Where is she?" Ava glanced around the empty kitchen toward the French doors that led out to the patio. She spotted Grace among the rest of the Calvano clan outside and started toward the door.

"Where are you going?" Joseph's voice stopped her. "She's over there."

Ava spun to find him pointing to the other side of the kitchen, where a small brown and white puppy sat blinking up at her.

"Princess?" She strode to the puppy and scooped her up. "You adopted her?" A twinge of envy went through her. As much as she'd known she couldn't have another puppy, she'd felt a sort of kinship with the little pup with the deformed leg.

"Nope." Joseph's grin grew into a chuckle. "You did."

"Me?" She stared at him and set the puppy down. "I told you, Aunt Lori would—"

"Disown you. I know. That's why I'm going to keep her for you. You can come visit her anytime you want."

Ava shook her head. That would mean spending way too much time with him.

"And that way you won't be able to avoid me forever." He echoed her thoughts.

"I haven't been avoiding you."

He gave her a look

Okay. She had been.

But it was for his own good—and hers.

They both turned as the French doors opened and Grace stepped inside.

Before Ava could say hello, Grace's arms wrapped her in a tight hug. "It's been too long."

Ava nodded, swallowing against the unexpected tears that gathered at the back of her throat. She hadn't realized how much she missed this family.

When they pulled apart, Grace gestured to Ava's camera bag. "We might want to get started on the pictures. Asher and Benjamin are making plans to toss Zeb into the river."

Ava laughed and followed Grace toward the door.

Outside was a glorious display of chaos as Asher and Benjamin chased Zeb, the others either looking on and laughing or ignoring the commotion as they carried on their conversations. Ava's heart filled at the sight of all the activity. This was how she remembered long summer days with the Calvanos as a kid—filled with chaos, laughter, and love. A place where she'd always felt like she belonged.

She raised a hand to cover her cheek, reminding herself that that had been before. She knew the Calvanos well enough to know none of them would judge her scars. But she didn't want them to pity her either.

A wolf whistle pierced the air, and Ava turned to Grace, impressed. Grace grinned at her as the activity and noise stopped.

"Y'all remember Ava, I'm sure."

"Hey, Ava." Asher jogged over and squished her in a hug. "Good to see you."

"Yeah. We've missed having you around." Benjamin was the next to hug her. She felt Joseph step closer.

Simeon and Zeb were on the far side of the patio but both raised a hand to wave.

"And you know Carly," Grace continued. Ava nodded as Carly stepped forward to hug her too. "And this is Simeon's wife Abigail. And you probably remember Ireland, Asher's fiancée. And Daddy, of course." Pastor Calvano crossed the patio and gave Ava the biggest hug of all. She wanted to tell him how sorry she was about Mrs. Calvano and about blowing off his calls, but now didn't seem like the time.

"Always good to welcome one of the family home," Pastor Calvano said quietly enough that Ava was pretty sure she was the only one who heard.

"Uh, Grace. I think you forgot someone." Joseph gestured to a man standing on the far side of the patio with Zeb and Simeon. "Ava, this is Grace's husband, Levi Donovan."

Levi stepped forward with a laugh. "You know you don't have to introduce me by my first and last name every time, right?" He held out a hand to Ava. "Just Levi."

Ava shook his hand. "Trust me. I would have known who you were even without the last name. Most people around here would, I reckon." Especially if they knew someone like Aunt Lori, who probably had every one of Levi's stats memorized.

"Well, everyone except Grace." Levi laughed as he pulled his wife to his side and planted a kiss on top of her head.

"Grace isn't like most people," Benjamin joked.

"Nope. That she isn't." Levi looked at Grace with such a tender expression that Ava had to look away.

Her eyes accidentally landed on Joseph, who was watching her with nearly the same expression.

She looked away from him as well and busied herself with her camera. "Should we get started?"

# Chapter 17

Joseph loved watching Ava work.

The way she took care in arranging his family for their portraits. The way she examined them like they were a fine work of art, even as they goofed around and jostled each other. The way she lifted the camera to her face like it was an extension of her arms.

But most of all, the way he could see how much she loved what she was doing.

"Hey, Joseph," she called, pulling the camera away from her face. "Would you mind looking at your daddy the way everyone else is?"

"Sorry." Joseph grinned, not sorry in the least. "I was looking at something else."

Next to him, Asher snorted. Well so what? He couldn't have hidden his feelings for Ava from his family if he tried. And right now, he really didn't want to try.

Everything felt so perfect, having Ava here. Like nothing had changed.

"A little more to the right, Joseph," Ava called.

"Like this?" Joseph shifted to the right, until he was directly behind Zeb, who stood a good two inches taller than him.

"Now I can't see you," Ava called, amusement coloring her tone. Or at least he chose to interpret it as amusement and not annoyance.

"I can fix that." Joseph bent his knees, then sprang onto Zeb's back. His brother let out a loud *oof* and staggered a few steps forward but didn't drop him.

"Y'all are impossible." But Ava was laughing as her camera clicked.

It took him by surprise every time, how much he loved the music of that laugh.

And how dedicated he was to making her do it again. Thankfully, it seemed easier in coming every time he saw her. Especially when there were puppies involved. He glanced to where Griffin and Tasha were playing, little Princess trying her best to keep up.

"Okay, one more spot." Ava glanced toward the river. "Joseph said you wanted to have a picture to honor your mama. I thought maybe we could do it around that rock by the river she always liked to sit on."

Joseph blinked as they all fell quiet. Mama used to call it her praying rock, and if you ever woke up early in the morning and didn't know where she was, she was sure to be sitting there, spending her time in conversation with the Lord.

"I'm sorry," Ava looked helplessly at the faces surrounding Joseph. "I didn't mean to– We don't have to–"

"That sounds like a really nice idea." Joseph managed to find his voice.

She sent him a relieved look as his siblings nodded.

"I think Mama would have liked that," Dad said, leading the way down the hill to the river.

Joseph took his time, letting the others get ahead of them before he fell into step next to her. "You remembered."

"I hope it's okay. I didn't mean to bring everyone down."

He let himself touch her elbow, only for a second. "It's perfect. Really."

Doubt still lingered in her eyes, but she bustled ahead of him to start positioning the others. When she got to him, he quietly took his place between Benjamin and Asher. Even he knew when it was time to be serious.

Ava studied them, then lifted her camera. His eyes followed her as she took shots from a few different angles, then declared the session done.

The others broke away, the somber atmosphere fading as they started to put a football game together.

Joseph held back, moving toward Ava, who was flicking through the pictures she'd just taken.

He stepped close enough to peer at them over her shoulder, letting himself be taken away on her rich, sweet jasmine scent.

Ava kept advancing through the pictures.

"I'll have to do some post-processing on them, adjust the light levels, but I think they'll turn out nice."

"I'm sure they will. You're very talented." He had to shove his hands in his pockets so he wouldn't rest them on her shoulders the way he used to. "Dad's grilling tonight. He told me to ask you to stay." Certainly, she wouldn't be able to resist an invitation from his father.

But she bit her lip.

"Grace made your favorite barbecue baked beans." Might as well sweeten the deal.

Ava's shoulders relaxed, and he knew he had her. But just to make sure: "And moon pies for dessert."

Ava shook her head but turned toward him. "You know me too well."

His eyes landed on hers. "Yes I do."

They stood like that for a moment, and he prayed she'd realize how true it was. He knew her better than he knew anyone, even himself.

For half a second, he thought he saw her waver.

"Joseph. Get over here." At Asher's shout, Ava looked away. Joseph could have smacked his brother.

Oblivious to what he'd interrupted, Asher was still yelling. "You're on my team."

"Sorry. They're impossible." He tried unsuccessfully to get Ava to look at him again.

"It's okay. Go play." Ava squatted to put her camera in her bag.

"I'd rather hang out with you." He probably shouldn't have said that out loud, even if it was true.

But instead of scolding him, Ava let her lips lift the slightest bit. "I'll watch."

"And you won't go anywhere? You'll stay for dinner?"

"You know you had me at moon pies." Ava's expression grew into a full smile. "I'm not going anywhere."

"Promise?"

She nodded and waved him off. "Promise. Now go."

He jogged toward his brothers, who were already huddling up. But he couldn't resist the urge to turn and look at Ava again. His heart nearly leapt right into the air when he found her watching him. He pointed two fingers at his eyes, then at her.

Though he couldn't hear her, he could see that she was laughing.

Turned out, her laugh looked as beautiful as it sounded.

# Chapter 18

Ava finished packing up her camera gear and threw her pack onto her back, then started up the hill to where the Calvano boys had a very loud game of football going on.

The predominant sound was laughter, and she rubbed at her cheek as it stretched into another smile.

She couldn't remember the last time she'd laughed so much.

It was probably before the fire.

No, it was definitely before the fire.

In fact, until Joseph had stepped back into her life a month ago, it'd been so long since she'd *really* laughed that she'd nearly forgotten how good it felt.

She stashed her camera bag in her vehicle, feeling Joseph's eyes on her as she moved around it. He again pointed to his eyes, then to her.

She laughed again and sent him a thumbs-up to say she got the message. He was watching. She couldn't break her promise not to leave.

Which was fine. Because she didn't want to be anywhere else.

Her camera gear safely stowed, Ava made her way to the front porch and settled onto the top step to watch the brothers play.

Joseph had always been quick on the field, and he didn't appear to have lost a step over the years, as he caught a long pass from Levi, then dodged past Zeb to run for the makeshift end zone before Simeon brought him down just shy of a touchdown. In spite of herself, Ava let out a quiet cheer.

An overwhelming sense of nostalgia overtook her.

How many Friday nights had she spent watching him play, cheering him on? How many Friday nights had she thought her life was perfect—she was head cheerleader, dating the football captain, both of their futures bright and full of promise?

After the game, they'd go to Murf's, share a shake, and talk about their plans for the future. He'd go to Cornell, and she'd only be a few hours away, modeling in New York. When he was done with school, they'd get married, have four kids and three dogs, and live happily ever after.

Never once in all those nights of planning had she stopped to consider what would happen if their dreams didn't come true. What would happen if one day, in the blink of an eye, everything changed.

"Mind if I join you?"

Ava shook herself out of her thoughts as Grace settled onto the step next to her.

"Just like old times, huh?"

Ava nodded. "Although they never had an NFL quarterback playing with them before. How did that happen?" Ava looked at Grace, who had always been unassuming and humble—the very last person she would have expected to marry a former football star.

Grace shifted to face her. "*That* is a very long story. But let's just say it all started with a prayer."

Ava lifted an eyebrow. "So, what? You prayed, 'God send me a football player,' and Levi Donovan showed up on your doorstep?"

"Actually, I said, 'Please not a football player.'" Grace laughed. "But God has a sense of humor."

Ava laughed along with her. Wasn't that how it always happened in movies? Two people who didn't seem meant to be together ended up discovering they were just right for each other.

But in the case of her and Joseph, it was the opposite: two people who had seemed so perfect for each other turned out not to be.

Or, well, one of them was still perfect. But the other was . . . not.

"What about you?" Grace bumped Ava's shoulder with hers. "Any prayers of your own?" Her gaze went pointedly to Joseph, who was picking himself up off the ground after tackling Zeb. He looked their way with a wave, but Ava didn't return it.

She shook her head, trusting that her makeup hid the flush she could feel rising to her cheeks. "No one."

Grace studied her a little too closely. "You know, he called me after you broke up with him. He was . . . I think devastated would be an understatement."

Ava pressed her lips together. Of course Joseph had been devastated. His girlfriend had been transformed from a model into a monster overnight.

"He kept telling me he was going to come see you whether you liked it or not. I told him to give you some time," Grace continued, apparently not sensing that this was the last thing in the world Ava wanted to talk about. "But I didn't mean eight years."

Ava shrugged. "It wouldn't have mattered."

"Wouldn't it?" Grace fell silent, and Ava hoped that meant she'd given up on the conversation.

They watched the game a few more minutes before Pastor Calvano called that the food was ready.

As they got up, Grace turned to her. "You know, Levi eventually got past my defenses. I hope you let Joseph get past yours."

# Chapter 19

Joseph stole another glance down the oversized patio table at Ava.

Somehow, during the course of the meal, he'd gone from sulking that his dad and Grace had taken the seats on either side of her to relishing the way she interacted with his family.

She threw her head back now and laughed at something Dad had said—hopefully not some embarrassing story from Joseph's childhood, though Ava knew most of those already—then glanced his way with a soft smile. He smiled back.

She had fit in like another member of this family when they were younger. He wanted her to remember that—to remember what it felt like to talk to his sister and to be teased by his brothers and to be welcomed by his father. Most of all, he wanted her to remember what it was like to be loved by him.

As he cleared the last bite from his plate, Joseph spotted Grace getting up from her seat, carrying her plate and glass with her. In an instant, he was on his feet, diving to claim her chair. He may not have minded Grace sitting next to Ava, but that didn't mean he wasn't going to claim that spot at the first opportunity.

"Hey." Ava's smile raced to his heart. "Your dad was just telling me about the job offer you got at Cornell."

He shrugged. He'd been honored, but it had been easy to turn down. "I wanted to be here."

Ava's eyes searched his face, and he prayed she'd see that she was a big part of the reason for that.

"Hey, y'all." Grace spoke from near the head of the table, and Ava's eyes swiveled to her. Joseph nearly growled at his sister for interrupting their moment. "I imagine you're wondering about the big news I mentioned."

Oh, that was right. In his anticipation of seeing Ava, Joseph had nearly forgotten that Grace had said she had news.

Grace shot a quick, nervous glance at her husband. Joseph caught the encouraging smile Levi offered, and his stomach plunged. Something was wrong, he could feel it.

"Are you going to tell us about your new coffee bar now?" he joked, trying to ease the sudden tension.

Grace's laugh was forced. "Maybe later. I put together a lecture just for you. But for now, I have news a little bigger than that."

"What's bigger than a coffee bar?" Joseph didn't know why he was so opposed to letting Grace continue. Only that he didn't want anything to mar this perfect evening.

"Joseph." Ava set a hand lightly on his. That shut him up.

Grace blew out a breath. "I don't really know how to say this, so I'm just going to come out and say it." She looked at Dad, who nodded, and Joseph's chest eased. If Dad already knew about it and didn't look worried, everything had to be fine.

"We have a sister." The words rushed from Grace's mouth.

Joseph stared at her. That was the big news?

"No kidding. You." This time the joke came from Benjamin.

Grace didn't laugh. "No. A half-sister. One we haven't met." She looked to Dad, who nodded for her to continue. "Mama told me before she went to the Lord. Before she and Daddy were married, she had a baby girl who she gave up for adoption."

"Hold on." Simeon spoke up from the small bistro table he shared with his wife. "You're saying Mama told you before she died? That was almost two years ago. Why are you just telling us now?"

Joseph looked from his brother to his sister, grateful Simeon's brain seemed to be processing faster than his own.

Grace nodded as if she'd been expecting the question. "I was hoping to wait until I had more information. All Mama could tell me was the baby's birthdate and that the name she gave her was Lydia. Mama gave me her blessing to search for her, but I haven't gotten anywhere, and I thought—"

"I don't believe this." Zeb jumped up from his seat. "Mama wasn't— She wouldn't have—"

"We all make mistakes, Zeb." Dad's voice was low. "Your mama confessed this one to me before she went home to heaven."

"And what? Y'all just wanted to drag her name through the mud now?"

"Zeb." Carly reached for his hand, but Zeb pulled away, stalking toward the house.

Carly gave them all an apologetic look and followed.

"This is not quite how I saw this going," Grace muttered.

"How did you see it going?" Simeon asked, with his characteristic calm counselor's voice.

"I don't know." Grace shrugged. "I just thought it was time for y'all to know. Thought maybe you might have some ideas I haven't thought of to search for her."

"What if she doesn't want to be found?" Ava's question was quiet, and she instantly popped a hand over her mouth. "I'm sorry. I didn't mean—" She gave Joseph a desperate look. "You know I wouldn't—"

"We know." Joseph took her hand. He still had no idea how he felt about what he'd just learned—but he did know he was grateful to have Ava here, at his side, for it.

"I've been checking adoption forums—places where people go if they're searching for their birth family. I thought I might have found something a few weeks back, but it turned out to be a dead end. That's when I realized that maybe it didn't matter if we never found her—y'all still needed to know she's out there. At the very least, we can pray for her, right?" Grace fell into her seat, and Levi leaned over to take her hand.

Which made Joseph realize that Ava's hand was still in his. He squeezed it and leaned closer. "Take a walk with me?"

"I should—" But her eyes landed on his, and she sighed. "Just a short one."

He let go of her hand so they could stand and clear their dishes.

On his way past Grace, Joseph squeezed her shoulder. "You did the right thing. Telling us."

Grace gave him a grateful smile. "You two have a nice walk."

They called the dogs, then started down the hill toward the river.

Without discussing it, they both turned left at the riverbank. They must have walked this way together a couple hundred times in their life.

"Well, that was unexpected. You doing all right?" Ava walked close enough that he could pick out her jasmine scent—but far enough away that it would have been awkward to try to take her hand again.

"Yeah. I think so. It's strange. I keep thinking about Mama. Did she ever regret not looking for her daughter? Did she ever wish she hadn't waited so long?"

He glanced at Ava, hoping she'd hear what he was really saying. That she'd understand he didn't want that kind of regret to happen to them.

"Sometimes there's healing in the waiting," Ava said finally.

Joseph watched the dogs frolic ahead of them as he contemplated that. "I suppose so. But sometimes waiting can become too comfortable. Paralyze us from moving forward. I wonder if that's what happened to Mama?" He wondered if it was what had happened to him. Had the eight years he'd waited to come back really been for Ava's sake? Or had it become too comfortable not to try? Not to let her reject him again?

"Mostly, I imagine she worried how y'all would react to learning she wasn't the person you thought she was," Ava said.

They both slowed as they came to the destination they'd been headed for, though neither of them had said it.

Their park.

It was so small—just a single slide, four swings, and an open, grassy area—that it didn't have a name.

But it was where they'd first met—so long ago that Joseph felt as if he'd known her forever. It was where they'd chased each other in epic games of freeze tag. And the rickety wooden pier that extended into the river was where they'd spent long, lazy teenage nights talking about their future.

Joseph gestured for Ava to follow him to it now. Maybe they could recapture the magic of those sweet, slow nights.

But the past eight years hadn't been kind to the pier. Water lapped in the spot where the first two planks should have been, and the end of the pier tilted at an odd angle.

Ignoring the pier, Griffin and Tasha splashed into the water, Princess taking one timid step behind them, then jumping back.

Ava scooped the puppy into her arms, nuzzling her face against the dog's neck. "Not ready for that yet, huh?"

But the puppy wiggled out of her arms and stepped into the water again, this time getting two paws wet before she backed up. Ava picked her up again, and the puppy nestled into her arms.

Joseph smiled. He wondered if Ava realized how very much like Princess she could be. He only hoped he'd be able to show her as much patience as Ava showed the puppy.

"Want to try it?" He pointed at the dilapidated pier.

At her nod, Joseph jumped easily over the missing planks. He stomped on the wood a few times to make sure it was solid, then turned and held out his hands so Ava could pass Princess to him. With the puppy wriggling in one hand, he held out his other hand to Ava.

She eyed it for a second, then reached for it.

The moment their skin made contact, it was as if all the years between the last time they'd been here and this moment had fallen away. Joseph let both the familiarity and the newness of her touch travel up his arm. This was how they were meant to be.

Too quickly, she landed next to him, pulling her hand out of his and taking Princess back.

He followed her to the edge of the pier, taking the side that angled closer to the water. He discarded his shoes and pulled off his socks as Ava slid out of her sandals. As they lowered themselves to the edge of the pier, Joseph scooted closer to her to avoid the spot where the planks tipped toward the water. The scent of her jasmine cloaked him, making him even more aware of her nearness. He kicked his feet in the river, letting the bite of the cooling water tingle through his toes. Ava's feet splashed next to his.

They sat in silence for a while, laughing every now and then at the big dogs' antics in the water as Princess curled up in Ava's lap and fell asleep.

Finally, Griffin and Tasha tired of swimming and trotted back to the riverbank.

"We should get back." But Ava didn't move as she said it.

Joseph turned toward her.

The last traces of light had bled from the sky, leaving them surrounded by a dusky blue. Maybe now, under the cover of darkness, was the time to ask the question that had burned in his mind for eight years. The reason, if he was honest, that he'd never worked up the courage to break his promise to let her go.

"Ava?" he whispered.

She turned to him, one hand going to her cheek. He lifted his hand to pull it away.

Then, still gripping her fingers in his, he forced the words out past his scorched throat. "Do you blame me for what happened?"

# Chapter 20

Ava was aware of every prick of cold in her toes, every slip of breeze against her cheek, every pulse of her heart in her throat, every nerve firing at the touch of Joseph's hand around hers.

Was that what he thought?

That she blamed him?

"Of course not," she whispered. Her fingers squeezed his before she pulled her hand back. She needed to get her senses under control. And more importantly, her heart. "I made the decision to go to that party. I knew Aunt Lori had said no, and—"

"And I was the one who asked you to go. Who convinced you it would be fine."

"No, Joseph." She gave him a stern look. It did no good to let him take the blame for what had happened. "I made my own decision."

She'd wondered a million times what would have happened if she hadn't gone that night. Would her life be normal now? Would *she* be normal? Would she and Joseph have gone on to live out their forever?

But questions like that would only drive her mad.

Joseph swallowed hard. "I thought that was why you broke up with me." He cleared his throat. "Because I let that happen to you."

Ava closed her eyes. She couldn't handle the guilt in his gaze—or the hope. "I never blamed you. I just didn't want you to see me like that." She opened her eyes, touching her fingers to the roughened skin of her cheek, hidden at the moment by makeup and darkness. "Like this."

Through the dark, she saw him lift his hand, but she didn't realize what he was doing until his fingers brushed against her skin.

No.

*No. No. No.*

She jerked her head out of his reach. It was enough that he'd seen her scars—she didn't need him to feel them too.

Joseph's hand fell into his lap. "You know that wouldn't have mattered to me." His voice was gentle. "I loved you for *you*. Not for your appearance."

Ava bit back her retort. That was easy enough to say, but what would have happened when he'd tried to kiss her and felt the uneven skin of her lips? Or when he'd tapped her nose and was repulsed by the missing pieces? What happened when he rolled over one morning expecting the face of an angel only to find a monster?

She refused to do that to him.

She refused to do that to herself.

That was why she'd broken up with him.

"You went to prom with Madison?" She didn't know where the question came from. She had promised herself never to ask it. Promised herself she didn't care. Promised herself it didn't matter.

Joseph puffed out a soft breath. "Yeah. Because I was angry with you." He gave a short laugh. "It was childish, but there it is."

Ava nodded. What else was there to say? They fell silent, listening to the night fill with the sounds of the river lapping the bank and the birds making their final calls of the evening.

"I didn't stay." Joseph's voice broke the stillness, making Ava jump. "I couldn't. I ran out on Madison the moment the first song started."

Ava lifted her head. "Why?"

“Because she wasn’t you.” Joseph scooted a little closer. “I got in my car and drove to your house, determined to pound on your door until you let me in.” He gazed past her, to the river. “But when I got there, I couldn’t do it.”

“I understand.” Ava had to stop to swallow. She’d known it would have been too much for him, seeing her like that. But it still hurt to have him confirm it.

“No. I don’t think you do.” Joseph drew his feet out of the water, then stood and paced the pier, a hand going to the back of his neck.

“I do.” There was no point in pretending it hadn’t happened. “I was hideous.”

“Do you really think that little of me?” The pulse of anger in Joseph’s voice took her by surprise. “You think I didn’t come in to see you because I was worried about how you looked?” He made a sound of disgust. “I thought you knew me better than that. I didn’t care. I would have—”

“That’s easy to say now, Joseph.” Anger pushed her to her feet as well, making Princess open her eyes and give a scolding look before snuggling back into Ava’s arms. “But the fact is that you didn’t get out of that car. You didn’t come in to see me.”

“Because you made me promise not to.” Joseph’s voice was nearly as quiet as the night.

Ava started to reply, then bit off her comment and ducked her head. She couldn’t deny that. He’d come to see her in the hospital, when her face was still wrapped in bandages, and all she could think as he’d looked at her was that she could never let him see what was under those bandages. Because once he did, he would never look at her the same way. So she’d told him she didn’t want to see him again. Had made him promise not to come again. To let her go.

And she’d thought he had.

No, she knew he had.

So why were they even having this conversation?

He shook his head. "The moment I made that promise, I knew it was a mistake. I should have fought harder for you, Ava. I shouldn't have let you convince me that us, apart, was best for anyone. I guess I was just scared."

Ava licked her rough lips. "It *was* best. I was setting you free. Letting you off the hook."

"I didn't want to be let off the hook, Ava." Joseph's voice rose. "I wanted to be there for you. Do you even remember what happened that night?"

Ava shook her head slowly. It had haunted her for years, the fact that she couldn't remember the moment that had changed her life forever. "I remember talking about the party with you and saying that I was going with or without Lori's permission. And I remember getting there and someone saying the bonfire was too small. But after that . . ." She let her words trail off. After that, everything was out of focus, like someone had messed with the lens of her memory.

Joseph stepped toward her. "Do you know how many times I've relived it?" His voice was low, his expression tortured. Somehow, it had never occurred to her that he might be troubled by memories of that night.

"Do you want me to tell you?" His voice was gentle, hesitant.

She stared past him toward the riverbank, contemplating. In some ways, it was easier not knowing. But in others, she felt like maybe knowing would give her the closure she had yet to find. She nodded slowly.

Joseph bent and pulled his shoes on. She watched him for a moment, then followed suit and tucked her feet into her sandals. Either he had changed his mind, or he wasn't going to tell her here.

Joseph straightened and took her hand, the warmth of his fingers sending a wild pulse through her wrist, and led her back toward shore. When they'd both jumped the missing planks, he led her to the grass and sat, pulling her down next to him. Princess stumbled off her lap, moseying over to sniff Griffin and Tasha.

"We were standing by the fire." Joseph sounded far away, like he was next to her but somewhere else at the same time. "You were cold. I didn't have a sweatshirt on, and you'd left yours in the car. So I said I'd go get it for you. I was only gone a few minutes, but . . ." He let out a loud breath, then swallowed.

"I came back to find people screaming and the fire blazing, like—" He squinted up at the sky. "Like some kind of inferno. I didn't understand it at first. Some of the flames were moving outside the fire pit. And then I heard someone scream, 'Help,' and even though it didn't sound like you at all, I knew it was you." His voice shook, and he ran his hands over his face. "You were on fire, Ava. It was the worst—" He cut off, shaking his head.

Ava had known that already, of course. She may not have remembered it, but she had gone through the operations and skin grafts and had the scars to prove it.

"Some genius had found a gas can and decided to make the fire bigger."

"I know," she whispered. "Some of the gas splashed onto me." That much the doctors had been certain of, based on the severity of her burns.

"I was out of my mind, Ava. To see you like that." Joseph turned toward her, and as much as she wanted to look away, she couldn't. "I ran across the yard and knocked you off your feet. I still remember the sound of your yell as you hit the ground. But you started rolling around, and I hit at the flames with the sweatshirt in my hands."

"I—" She swallowed hard. No one had ever told her that Joseph had been the one to save her. In fact, no one had ever told her much of anything about that night. Aunt Lori had always insisted that she needed to focus on getting better, not on what had happened. "Thank you."

"I don't want your thanks." Joseph gave her a long look. "I want you to know that I saw you, Ava. At that moment. When your skin was falling off and blistered, and you didn't look anything like you anymore."

Ava closed her eyes. She didn't want to think of him seeing her like that.

"And you know the only thought I had?"

Ava shook her head. She wasn't sure she wanted to know, but she was powerless to tell him to stop.

"I thought, 'Please, Lord, let her live, so I can tell her that I love her.'"

Ava lifted her head, letting herself meet his eyes for a second before dropping her gaze to her lap. She ran a finger back and forth over the long ridge that sliced diagonally across the top of her left hand. She should say something—respond to that somehow.

She let out a long breath. "We should go."

Joseph was silent, but finally she heard him stir and push to his feet. "Yeah. Okay."

She got up too, careful to keep her distance as they called for the dogs.

"I'm sorry." A heavy sigh seeped out of Joseph, so different from his usual goofball self that it made Ava's heart ache. "I shouldn't have told you."

"No." Ava let herself touch the back of his hand for a moment. "I'm glad you did."

Even if she had no idea what to do with it.

# Chapter 21

"Good morning." Aunt Lori was whistling as she wiped down the counter Sunday morning. "I just put a roast in the slow cooker for tonight. Michael's coming for dinner."

That made the third time in the past week. Not that Ava minded. Mr. Germain was kind and funny and obviously deliriously in love with Aunt Lori.

*Love.*

The word rattled her. It was the same word Joseph had used last night.

"Why didn't you tell me Joseph was the one who saved me?"

Aunt Lori stopped wiping the counter and dried her hands against her shirt. "I didn't know at first. No one seemed to."

Ava ran a finger over the scar lines on her hand. "At first?"

Lori shrugged. "One of the kids who was at the party told me a couple months later. But by then, you two had already broken up, and it seemed cruel to tell you." She frowned. "I always did mean to thank him for that, but I was too mad at him for the way he left. I guess I owe him an apology."

"Oh." Ava wasn't sure what else to say, except that she supposed she did too.

"Are you going to church?" Lori gestured to the ankle-length blue dress Ava had chosen this morning. "Or do you have a date?"

"Definitely not a date," Ava said dryly. "I thought I might try to go to church." The more time she'd spent reading her Bible, the more she'd realized how much she hungered for God's Word. And how much she missed going to church. "Do you want to come with me?" She knew the question was pointless, but still, you never knew what might happen.

Lori's head shake was instant, just as Ava had known it would be.

"I'll see you later then." But as she turned toward the door, the question she'd wanted to ask a thousand times as a kid wouldn't leave her alone. "Why don't you ever go to church?"

Lori started emptying the dishwasher, and Ava was sure her aunt was going to blow her off. But then Lori said, "I don't like feeling not good enough."

"What do you mean?" Ava tilted her head, studying her aunt, trying to understand.

Aunt Lori sighed. "You don't remember your grandparents."

Ava shook her head. Her grandfather had died before Ava was born, her grandmother when Ava was only a year old.

"They were really strict. And really critical," Lori continued. "If I put one toe out of line, they jumped all over me and told me how evil and wicked I was. So I don't really feel like going to church and hearing what a bad person I am all over again."

Ava swallowed. That wasn't her experience of church at all. But who was she to talk? She hadn't been to church in years.

Still, she should know how to respond to that. "Well," she said lamely, "If you ever change your mind . . ."

Lori smiled at her. "Not likely. Now go, before you're late."

Ava hesitated a second longer, then stepped out the front door, ordering an offended-looking Griffin to stay. The morning was cool, a light fog wrapping the trees in a gossamer veil.

Ava pulled in a long breath, catching a hint of dried leaves and earth.

Was she ready for this?

Only one way to find out.

She got into her vehicle and headed for town, trying not to relive those moments at the pier last night. Trying not to see the fear in Joseph's eyes as he'd talked about seeing her on fire. Trying not to hear the brokenness in his voice when he'd relived the way she'd sent him away.

Had it been a mistake? Should she have let him stay, let him be with her through those terrible days? Let him see her at her worst?

She shook her head as she slowed for a stop sign. That would have been selfish. It was better this way, letting him go. Letting him find someone else—someone whole.

*He didn't find someone else.* The thought that had been hanging on the fringes of her hopes sneaked past the barrier she'd tried to erect. *He came back.*

Ava sighed as she pulled into the parking lot of Beautiful Savior. Thinking like this wasn't going to get her anywhere.

It wasn't until she'd parked and turned off the car and started walking toward the door that she noticed all the people. So many people.

She froze right there in the middle of the sidewalk.

She couldn't go forward.

She couldn't turn around and flee.

Her heart thundered in her throat, and her breath sliced her chest in short, sharp gasps.

If she went in there, she was going to have another panic attack for sure.

Somewhere in the distance, she thought she heard someone call her name. But she couldn't turn her head to look. She tried to concentrate on breathing, the way her counselor had taught her. But her chest was too tight, her lungs too small. She was going to suffocate right here in front of church.

"Ava." Someone said her name again, closer, and then Joseph's face swam into view. "I'm so glad you— Are you okay?" Warm hands clasped around her icy ones. "What can I do?"

"I can't—" she gasped out. "Breathe."

"Yes you can." Joseph's hands tightened around hers. "We can breathe together." He sucked in a loud breath, then blew it out through his mouth.

Ava focused on the sound, on the up and down of his shoulders, on the calm reflecting from him. After a moment, she felt her inhales and exhales matching his.

"Good." His eyes were locked on hers, his breaths still audible.

They were still breathing in tandem as the church bell chimed from the steeple.

Ava glanced over Joseph's shoulder as the panic pushed forward again.

"Hey, look at me." Joseph shifted so his face was in front of hers again. "Don't worry about the bell. We'll go in when you're ready. Or we won't. It's completely up to you."

Ava pulled in a few more breaths, each one coming more easily than the last.

Finally, she let out a long exhale. "I think I'm ready."

"We don't have to." Joseph stepped closer to her. "We can try again another time."

But she shook her head. For some reason she couldn't explain, the near panic attack had left her wanting to go inside even more. Or maybe it was knowing Joseph would be with her.

Joseph let go of one of her hands but kept his grip firmly on the other as he pivoted to stand next to her.

Ava tried to tell herself to pull her hand away. But right now, she needed every ounce of strength he could lend her.

When they reached the church doors, he turned to her. "What made you come today?"

She glanced at the stained glass window above the door, considering. "I felt like I needed . . . something." She wished she could explain it better than that, but Joseph's smile was understanding.

"I have a feeling this is the place to find it." He ushered her inside, where the congregation was already singing the first hymn.

Ava's eyes went to the packed sanctuary, and she had to fight off a renewed flare of panic. She'd forgotten that the Calvanos always sat in the third pew from the front.

"How about we sit in the balcony?" Joseph leaned closer, his whisper fluttering a strand of her hair. "There's never anyone up there."

"What about your family?" If there was one thing the Calvanos were known for, it was that they were a close-knit family. She'd always loved sitting with them at church, feeling like she belonged with them. But today, the thought of walking up there, past all those people . . . she just couldn't.

"They'll be fine without me. Come on." He tugged her toward the left side of the entryway, where stairs led up to a small balcony.

He was right—they were the only ones up there, aside from the organist. As they sat, Joseph readjusted his grip so that their fingers interlocked. Ava clutched his hand tighter as the song came to an end and Pastor Calvano began the first Scripture reading. As the service went on, she found herself relaxing. The flow of the service—the readings, the prayers, the songs—was familiar and brought a kind of comfort she hadn't experienced in a long time.

When Pastor Calvano moved to the pulpit to deliver the sermon, Ava let herself sit back, her shoulder lightly brushing Joseph's. Even as a kid she'd always loved listening to Pastor Calvano as he preached, the lilting up and down of his words seeming to wrap her up in God's love as he spoke.

She wondered if it was possible to feel that way again. Or were things too different now? Was *she* too different now?

"Children of God," Pastor Calvano began, and Ava smiled at the familiar greeting he'd used for every sermon she'd ever heard him preach. "How do you feel about having your picture taken?" He glanced around the church as a few people groaned.

Ava was torn. She refused to have her own picture taken—for obvious reasons—but her livelihood depended on others wanting to have photos of themselves and their loved ones.

"I only ask," Pastor Calvano continued, "because family picture day was always my wife's favorite day. Mine, not so much. Which is probably why I've put off getting them done since she went home to the Lord."

Ava squeezed Joseph's hand tighter, regretting once again that she hadn't been there for him through that.

"But when my son came to me last week and said we should get some new family pictures taken, I reluctantly agreed."

Ava leaned closer to Joseph. "Which son?"

He shrugged but grinned a little.

"You? Why?" Everyone knew Joseph hated having his picture taken.

This time he looked at her full on, and she saw the answer in his eyes. He had wanted to spend time with her.

She swallowed and turned her attention back to the sermon.

"We had a great photographer," Pastor Calvano was saying, and Ava could have sworn he looked up into the balcony for a second. She ducked her head as Joseph nudged her shoulder.

"But—" Pastor Calvano held up a hand. "I can tell you that there's one thing about those pictures I'm not going to like. Wouldn't like no matter who took them."

Ava stiffened. He hadn't even seen the images yet. How could he know he wouldn't like them?

Pastor Calvano patted his somewhat rounded middle. "They're going to show this."

Ava relaxed as a laugh sounded through the congregation. *That* she couldn't be blamed for, though she'd done her best to pose him in ways that minimized his tummy somewhat.

"I'm hoping maybe she can do some magic with Photoshop to make me look better. Maybe give me a body-builder body." He lifted an arm to make a muscle, and next to her Joseph groaned quietly, whispering, "Really, Dad?"

Now it was Ava's turn to nudge him. No matter how much he complained, she knew he secretly loved it when his daddy acted all embarrassing for the sake of the Gospel.

"What about you?" Pastor Calvano continued. "What do you see when you look at a picture of yourself? Do you see your wrinkles, maybe your thinning hair?" He patted his own sparse follicles. "Your scars?"

Ava sucked in a breath. In her case, they were hard to miss.

"And those are just the physical imperfections," Pastor Calvano added. "We can go deeper too. What about mental imperfections? Are you bad at math? A terrible speller? Not so great at geography?"

Ava turned to make a face at Joseph, who had once thought Tennessee was its own country. He stuck his tongue out at her.

"And let's go deeper still," Pastor Calvano was saying. "How about the spiritual imperfections? Is all you see when you look at yourself your sins? All the times you've done what you know is wrong? The times you've failed to do what was right?"

Pastor Calvano paused, letting it sink in.

"Makes a pretty ugly picture, doesn't it?" This time his pause was longer, and Ava shifted in her seat.

"You ever wonder why God chose you?" Pastor Calvano went on. "I mean, surely there are people out there who are prettier, smarter, kinder, better than you, right?"

Ava didn't mean to scan the congregation below. Didn't mean for her eyes to fall on the back of Madison's head. She looked away.

"I mean, he's *God*," Pastor Calvano continued. "He could have anyone he wants. So why would he pursue *you*? Why would he want *me*, with all my faults and failures, my flabby abs and bald head and terrible spelling and filthy sins?"

Pastor Calvano paused, and a shiver went through Ava. Joseph's hand moved in hers, lacing her fingers tighter.

"Oh beloved," Pastor Calvano's voice was tender. "Don't you see? God doesn't love you *in spite of* all of those things. He loves you because he has erased all of those things. He didn't just go in with Photoshop and touch you up a little here and a little there. No, he changed your *whole picture* with the blood of Jesus. He has erased every last trace of sin, every last imperfection, and he has made you perfect in him." Pastor Calvano's words struck at Ava.

Perfect was not a concept she understood anymore.

"The next time you look at a picture of yourself," Pastor Calvano said, "do me a favor and see it as God does—an image of his masterpiece, redeemed from sin, created to love and serve him. 'Like clay in the hand of the potter, so you are in my hand,' God says. Remember that. Amen."

It took Ava a moment to realize that Joseph was tugging her to her feet as the congregation stood to pray. She closed her eyes and tried to pay attention to the prayer. But her thoughts were stuck on that image. Clay in the hands of a potter.

The only problem was, clay broke, just like that pot she had made in VBS.

And though Joseph may have glued the clay pot back together, she wasn't sure there was anything that would ever be able to restore her broken pieces.

Joseph made himself let go of Ava's hand as the church service ended. He had wanted it to go on forever, not only because it gave him an excuse to hold Ava's hand but because he had felt the message working in her—felt the way she had relaxed when his dad talked about God wanting each and every one of them. Now if only she could see that Joseph wanted her too. That he loved her too.

"Ready to go?" he asked reluctantly.

Ava's gaze drifted to the pews below, to the people filing slowly out of the church, stopping to laugh and chat with each other.

"I'm sorry." She ducked her head. "I know it's silly, but . . . Would you mind if we waited until it clears out a little?"

Mind spending a few more minutes with her?

No, in fact, he did not mind that at all.

"We can wait." He leaned back in his seat, debating whether he should tell her the words he'd stayed up all night rehearsing.

"Look, Ava." He sat forward suddenly, making her jump. "I'm sorry. About last night. I never should have told you. I just . . ."

He had just needed her to know that that night at the bonfire hadn't affected only her. That it had hurt him more than he could say to see her go through that and then to have her push him away.

But maybe that had been selfish. She clearly carried her own scars from that day—and not only on her skin. She shouldn't have to carry his too.

She didn't look at him but peered across the church toward the cross that hung above the altar. "I needed to know. I'm glad you told me."

"Is that why you ran away?" When he'd put his heart right out there.

She turned to him, her expression surprised. "I wasn't running away. I was . . . processing some things. It was a lot to take in." She pushed to her feet, gesturing to the empty sanctuary below. "I think we can go now."

Joseph followed, trying to decide how much time she was going to need to process and whether she could eat lunch while doing it.

He was about to ask her when Dad appeared at the bottom of the steps.

"Ava." Dad's voice was warm. "It's so good to see you here. I hope I didn't offend you, talking about pictures like that."

Ava's laugh was equally warm. "I wasn't offended at all. You gave me a lot to think about."

"I find God's Word always does." Dad loosened his tie. "You should come by for lunch."

Joseph hid a grin. Sometimes he really loved his dad.

"Oh, I couldn't," Ava protested. "You just fed me last night."

Dad shrugged. "Well, I have it on good authority that there are plenty of moon pies left, but if you don't want any . . ."

"All right. All right." Ava held up her hands. "You Calvanos are terrible. You know all my weaknesses."

"Maybe." Dad winked at her. "But we'd only ever use them for good. Right, Joseph?"

Joseph nodded. "Yes, sir." As long as good meant him and Ava together, he was in complete agreement.

# Chapter 22

"Nervous, girl?" Joseph rubbed behind Tasha's ears as the Samoyed panted up at him after their run Saturday morning, while Princess explored the flower bed nearby.

Today was the day of the big test. Ava would be here in a few minutes, along with her friend who tested therapy dogs for licensing.

But it wasn't the test Joseph was nervous about.

After lunch last Sunday, he'd convinced Ava to work with him and Tasha—and she'd come over Tuesday night and Thursday night to work some more.

So he was confident that Tasha was ready.

What he was less confident about was where he stood with Ava. She wasn't as standoffish as she'd been in the beginning—and every once in a while, he almost thought he saw a longing for more in her gaze. But then it would pass, and she would retreat. At this rate, they'd both be in a nursing home before she was willing to date him again.

It'd be worth the wait.

*Unless she never says yes.*

That wasn't a possibility he was willing to consider.

As a vehicle turned onto their street, Tasha's ears perked, Princess toddled out of the flower bed, and Joseph sat up straighter. All three of them watched as Ava's silver SUV approached.

Joseph stood as she pulled into the driveway but restrained himself from following Tasha and Princess to the vehicle. He was learning that he needed to give Ava space, especially when they first saw each other again after a day or two apart.

Griffin jumped out first, sniffing Tasha and Princess before running to Joseph's side. He bent to pet the dog, scratching the spot on his neck that always made Griffin drop to the ground and flip over for a belly rub. He would never understand why God couldn't have created people to be as easy to understand as dogs were.

Ava stepped out of the vehicle and swept Princess into her arms. "Well, hello puppy. Did you grow again? It's only been two days. Jacqueline just called. She's running late but should be here in a few minutes."

It took Joseph a moment to realize that the last part of her statement was directed to him.

"Okay." He didn't know what else to say, so he simply allowed himself to watch her, to enjoy the way her entire demeanor softened as she nuzzled Princess.

"Have you been working on 'leave it' with Tasha?" Ava set Princess down.

"Yes ma'am." That was still Tasha's biggest weakness—leaving food behind when commanded. She was more of an eat-it-first-and-ask-questions-later kind of dog. But they'd been working on it every day, and she could almost always do it now.

"All right. Let's try it." Ava reached into her pocket and pulled out a handful of Tasha's favorite beef treats.

"That's not fair." Joseph eyed his dog, who had already picked up the scent of the treats and trotted over to sniff Ava's hand. "That's like putting a steak on the ground and expecting me not to go for it."

Ava's sudden laugh took him by surprise, and he gladly joined in. This was more like it. More like them.

She was still smiling as she placed the treats on the ground two feet in front of Tasha.

Instantly, the dog was moving toward them.

"Leave it," Joseph ordered.

Tasha took one more tentative step, then stopped, giving him a disbelieving look over her shoulder.

"Good girl." He grinned and stepped forward to pet her. She leaned into him, then gave the treat one more regretful look.

"Okay. Get it." At Ava's words, Tasha dove for the treat.

"I told you." He elbowed Ava as she stood. "We're ready."

"Good." Ava elbowed him back, a familiar playfulness to the gesture that filled Joseph with relief. She was coming around. "Because Jacqueline is here."

After Ava had introduced the gray-haired woman who would be testing Tasha, they got started. Jacqueline asked him to walk Tasha on a leash, hold her still while Jacqueline touched her side and feet and tail, and walk Tasha past Griffin without letting her get distracted. Finally, she set a treat on the ground, telling Joseph to order the dog to leave it.

The whole time he worked with Tasha, Joseph could feel Ava's eyes on him. Every once in a while, he dared to glance at her. And each time, he could swear her expression had melted a little more, until it resembled something closer to . . . tenderness, maybe. Or was he projecting his own feelings onto her?

He'd have to sort that out later.

For now, Jacqueline was talking to him. Or, to Tasha, really.

She was kneeling at the dog's side. "You, young lady, are going to make a wonderful therapy dog. You're so soft, I bet you'll be everyone's new favorite." She pushed to her feet and held out a hand to Joseph. "Congratulations. You, sir, are now the proud owner of a licensed therapy dog." She signed a piece of paper on her clipboard and passed it to him.

"Thank you." But his eyes went instantly to Ava. She was smiling, her hands clasped in front of her.

Would it be too much to give her a celebratory hug?

Probably.

He'd have to settle for smiling back at her.

"So—" Jacqueline was still talking, and he forced his attention to her. "Your first three visits need to be observed by one of our testers. Normally, I would offer, but I'm moving next week, so maybe Ava could . . ."

Joseph's gaze swung to Ava.

Her smile nearly stopped his heart. "I'm going to the Children's Hospital this afternoon, actually. We can go together."

Joseph swallowed.

Today?

As much as his heart was doing high jumps at the thought of spending the day with Ava, he wasn't sure he was ready for the Children's Hospital. He'd never been as comfortable around people as he was around animals.

"This afternoon is good," he heard himself say.

"Great." Jacqueline headed for her car. "Congratulations again." And then she was gone, leaving Joseph feeling somehow more nervous than he had before the test.

He blew out a breath, turning to Ava. "Wow. I can't believe we did it."

"I can." Ava stepped closer. "How about some lunch before we go? My treat."

Joseph gaped at her. Was she asking him on a date?

"Or otherwise I can come back and . . ." Ava faltered, and Joseph realized that he'd been so stunned he hadn't answered her question.

"No. I mean, yes. I mean, let's get lunch." He was practically stumbling over himself trying to answer, and he didn't care. "Where do you want to go?"

"Murf's again? I think they deliver, so we wouldn't have to . . . what?"

He was giving her a strange look. "You still don't like going out in public, do you?"

She shrugged. "It's no big deal. I just figured that way we didn't have to worry about what to do with the dogs." But her hand strayed to her cheek, and he wondered if she realized she did that every time she felt self-conscious.

"Okay." Far be it from him to argue against spending more time alone with her. "I'll call and order."

They played fetch with the dogs until their order arrived, then took their food out to the back patio. When they were almost done eating, Ava looked at him strangely. "You're being oddly quiet."

Joseph laughed. "I didn't know I was usually that loud."

But Ava was still looking at him in that way that said she knew something was up. He crumpled the wrapper from his burger and stuck it in the bag. "What do I say to them?"

He kept his eyes on the yard, but he could feel Ava still watching him. "Say to who?"

"The sick kids." He shoved a hand through his hair, letting himself look at her for a second. "I'm better with animals."

"Well, what would you say to a sick animal?"

Joseph glanced at Tasha, Griffin, and Princess, all three of whom were staring up at Ava, who still had a bite of burger in front of her. "I don't know. 'Good boy' or 'good girl.'"

"Yeah, don't say that to the kids." Ava poked his arm. "You're going to be fine, Joseph. I know you don't think so, but you happen to be pretty good with people."

"I am?" That was news to him. But it didn't answer his question. "But really, what am I supposed to say to them?"

"It might help not to think of them as a *them*." Ava's gaze shifted to the yard. "They're just kids, like any other kids. Tell them about Tasha or about being a vet. Ask them about their favorite animals. All they want is a chance to be kids, you know? To laugh a little. To not think about being sick or hurt for a while. To not think about being different."

"Is that how you felt?" Joseph inched closer. He hated to imagine her going through all of that without him.

"Sometimes, yeah." She opened her mouth as if to say more, then closed it again.

"What?"

She shrugged, not looking at him. "Sometimes I still do."

Joseph touched her hand, just long enough to let her know he was there.

That no matter what, he would always be there.

"You like him."

Ava glanced in surprise at the teen girl petting Griffin.

When Brianna had separated herself from the other children gathered around Tasha and Joseph in the hospital playroom, Ava had come to sit with her. But this was the first time the girl had spoken.

"Who? Griffin? He's a good dog." Ava patted his side.

But Brianna rolled her eyes. "Dr. Joseph. You've been watching him the whole time."

Ava pulled her eyes off Joseph. "I'm his observer. It's my job."

"Oh. Your *job*." Brianna smirked.

Ava worked to keep her gaze from straying back to Joseph. But it really *was* her job to observe him and Tasha.

He'd been stiff for the first few minutes as she'd introduced him, but the moment the kids had started petting Tasha, he'd warmed up to them with ease.

Now they were gathered around him as he promised to show off Tasha's tricks.

"Tasha, roll over," Joseph ordered.

Ava watched with interest. As far as she knew, Tasha had never learned that command.

Tasha took one look at Joseph—and lifted her paw to shake.

Joseph threw his hands in the air. "Seriously, Tasha?"

The kids roared with laughter, and Ava chuckled along.

"See," Brianna crowed. "You like him."

"What?" Ava grinned at her. "I thought it was funny."

But as Joseph commanded Tasha to stand on two legs, the kids dissolving into giggles when the dog laid down instead, Ava had to admit that her heart was pounding hard against the door of the safe she'd locked it in.

It didn't help that Joseph looked up and grinned at her right at that moment.

Next to her, Brianna snickered.

Ava turned to her. "Oh yeah, smarty pants, and is there a boy you like? Maybe the one who sent this?" She plucked a hand-drawn card out of Brianna's fingers, examining the intricate sketch of a hummingbird hovering over a flower.

"That's from my mom." But the blush on Brianna's cheeks gave her away.

"Your mom, huh?" Ava popped the card open and peeked at the signature. "I didn't realize your mom was named Wyatt."

She laughed as Brianna snatched the card from her fingers and hugged it to herself.

But the girl's face grew serious. "They said I'm going to lose my hair."

Ava nodded. A lot of the kids here were bald as they went through various stages of cancer treatment.

"So it doesn't pay to like anyone," Brianna added, slapping the card face-down on her lap.

"That's not true." Ava set a hand on top of the girl's. "Your hair will grow back." Unlike her scars—those were permanent. "And in the meantime, I know you can rock the bald look. Or try out some cute wigs or chemo caps. Wyatt will be crazier about you than ever."

"Yeah right. He's probably already forgotten about me."

Ava frowned at her. "Is he a good guy?"

"Yeah."

"And does he like you?"

Brianna's smile was shy. "I think so."

"Then I wouldn't worry." Ava glanced again toward Joseph, who was now fielding questions from the kids. "The good ones tend to stick around."

# Chapter 23

"Today was . . . not what I expected." Joseph turned to Ava as he shifted the car into park in her driveway. His heart was full of so many things that he couldn't put into words right now.

"Is that a good thing or a bad thing?" Ava gave him a teasing smile.

But for once, he was feeling serious. "Thank you. I never would have done this if it weren't for you."

And he would have been missing out. Those kids had been so amazing. And hearing them laugh—it was now his second-favorite sound, after only Ava's.

"You're welcome." Ava's eyes grew serious too.

He searched her face, trying to figure out what she was thinking.

Griffin popped his head up and poked his nose against Ava's shoulder, breaking whatever it was that had been building between them.

"So. I guess I'll see you." He wanted to ask *when* he would see her, but he didn't want to push her.

She swallowed. "Do you want to come in? We could make a pizza or . . ."

"Yeah." The surprise and delight in his voice were anything but subtle, but he didn't care. "I'd like that."

He turned off the engine and opened his door, jumping out before she could take the invitation back.

He let the dogs out of the backseat, then joined her on the short path that led to the front door. A sudden swoop of nerves went through him.

*Don't mess this up.*

Ava wanted to be friends. She'd invited him in for pizza as friends.

And as much as he might pray that just friends would someday become something more, he needed to remember his promise to her.

Inside, Ava pulled out a frozen pizza and held it up. "I know your mama wouldn't approve, but it's all I've got."

Joseph laughed. He loved that Ava knew so much about his family. About his mama. "If you want to know a secret, Mama was known to make a frozen pizza now and then too."

"No." Ava pressed a hand to her heart, as if scandalized. "Say it ain't so."

"I remember this one time. She was trying to pass off these frozen pizzas as homemade, because she didn't want us to know. Only Simeon had found the packaging in the trash, so we all told her how much better the pizza was than usual. By the end of the meal, she was so mad." A pang of sadness cut at his heart even as he laughed. He sure could use Mama's advice right now. He was sure she'd have plenty of it.

"You miss her." Ava paused on the other side of the counter.

Joseph rubbed at his jaw. "Sometimes I forget she isn't here anymore, you know? I pick up my phone to call her about something, and it takes a minute to realize why her number isn't in it."

He'd never told that to anyone else, and he felt oddly vulnerable. He wondered if that was how Ava felt all the time, with her wounds so visible to everyone she met.

"Joseph, I'm so sorry." Ava reached across the counter and set her hand on his. "I promise the sharpness of the grief gets ground down eventually. And when it becomes softer around the edges, the memories get easier too."

Joseph nodded as his eyes went to her hand resting on top of his. With his other hand, he traced a finger slowly across the line of scars on the back of it.

Ava's hand twitched, but she didn't pull away.

He lifted his eyes to hers. "Ava, I—"

"What would you like to drink?" She yanked her hand out from between his.

Joseph kicked himself. He was going too fast for her. Even if it felt slower than a turtle stuck on its back.

"Water is fine, thanks." He stood and walked to the picture windows in the adjoining family room. He needed a little space so he wouldn't do something else he shouldn't, like wrap her in his arms and kiss her until she knew—right down to her soul—that he wasn't giving up on her. On them.

"Here you go." Ava padded up next to him, standing well back as she passed the glass of water.

He took a long drink, searching for something safe to say. "It looked like you were having a good conversation with that girl at the hospital today."

"Brianna?" Ava sighed. "It was good talking to her. She's worried her hair is going to fall out. From her chemo."

"Oh." The things some of these kids had to go through sat heavy on Joseph's heart. He wondered if he'd be able to handle trials like that if he had to.

"There's a boy she likes," Ava continued. "And she thinks he won't like her without hair."

"What'd you tell her?" Joseph's question was so quiet, he barely heard it himself.

But Ava took the slightest step toward him. "I told her the good ones tend to stick around." Her smile was soft and gentle and full of more meaning than he could handle.

He took the smallest step toward her too. "Ava."

He lifted a hand to her unscarred cheek.

She looked up at him with those big green eyes—the same eyes he'd known nearly his entire life—and he was lost.

"Joseph." Her whisper was almost his undoing.

The need to kiss her was so strong that he only barely managed to stop himself.

But she'd made it clear that she wasn't ready for a relationship with him. And until she told him otherwise, he needed to respect that.

He withdrew his hand and took a step backwards.

Confusion wrinkled Ava's brow as she watched him.

"I'm sorry, Ava. I didn't—"

The timer on the oven dinged, making both of them jump.

Joseph caught a flicker of hurt on Ava's face before she scurried past him toward the kitchen. He let out a long, slow breath, kneading his fists into the back of his neck.

Was she hurt because he'd almost kissed her—or because he hadn't?

Ava played with the pizza crumbs on her empty plate. Across from her, Joseph did the same.

Neither of them had said more than a dozen words as they'd eaten, although the weight of all the words they weren't saying hung heavy between them.

They'd almost kissed.

She couldn't deny that—because as much as she tried to pretend it hadn't happened, her lips insisted on continually imagining what it would have felt like to have his pressed against them for the first time in eight years.

It was fortunate that he'd had the sense to pull back. Because she'd gotten so caught up in the moment that she'd almost let her heart break free.

*But why?* That was the question that wouldn't stop pecking at her brain. *Why had he pulled back?*

Surely, he must have been able to tell that she wanted the kiss too.

Unless—

Unless he didn't want it.

Unless, when it came down to it, the thought of kissing her scarred lips had repulsed him.

She ran a finger over them, then quickly dropped her hand. No need to call attention to them.

Joseph cleared his throat. "Thanks for the pizza."

She nodded as he got up and carried his plate to the sink.

"I should, uh—" He looked around the room—everywhere but at her. "I should get going. Princess probably needs to go out, and . . ."

"Yeah." Why did the thought of him leaving make her feel so deflated?

But she got up to walk him to the door.

He called for Tasha, who looked up from her spot next to Griffin on the couch, clearly asking *already*?

Ava had to agree with her. Did they really have to go already?

She considered asking if he wanted to watch a movie. But she knew that would be a bad idea. She'd be too tempted to slide close and snuggle into his arms, the way she used to.

"Tasha, come!" His voice was more urgent now. It couldn't be more obvious that he couldn't get out of here fast enough.

Ava stepped onto the porch with him, letting the cool evening air wash over her.

"Thank you again for today." Joseph turned to her, his gaze holding her captive.

Oh my stars. Why did he again look like he was going to kiss her? Had she misunderstood his hesitation earlier? And more importantly, did she want him to kiss her for real this time?

The seconds passed between them, and neither moved. Joseph's arm twitched, and Ava's breath hitched. Was he going to wrap it around her?

But instead he lifted his hand to shield his eyes as a bright light swung over his face and tires crunched on the driveway.

Ava let out a breath. "Lori's home."

Joseph took a step back, rubbing his hand over the top of his head. "Yeah."

They both turned toward the driveway as Lori's car door slammed. But instead of her customary speedy pace, Lori dragged her feet toward the porch.

Ava thought at first it was because she didn't want to interrupt whatever she thought was going on between her and Joseph. But as Aunt Lori stepped closer, Ava caught a glimmer on her cheeks.

Tears?

Ava had only ever seen Aunt Lori cry once—when she'd told Ava about her parents' deaths—but she'd never forgotten it.

"Lori?" she stepped toward her aunt.

Lori jumped and swiped a quick hand over her cheeks. "Sorry. I didn't see you two out here. I'll get out of your way."

She sped up, but Ava grabbed her arm. "Are you okay?"

Lori nodded, but an abrupt sob burst out of her. "Sorry." She shook off Ava's hand. "I'm fine." She ran up the steps and into the house.

"What in the world?" Ava looked helplessly from the door to Joseph.

He gave her a sympathetic look. "Guess I'd better let you deal with that." He touched a hand to her arm. "Goodnight, Ava." He gave her a long look, then jogged to his car.

"Goodnight," she whispered into the empty darkness as his car disappeared down the driveway. She longed to sink onto the porch steps and contemplate what had just passed between them. But that would have to wait for later.

Right now, she had to find out what was wrong with Aunt Lori.

# Chapter 24

"Lori?" Ava called tentatively as she closed the door softly behind her.

"In the kitchen." Lori's voice sounded completely normal, and Ava frowned. There was no way she'd imagined the tears on her aunt's face.

She shrugged at Griffin, and the two of them made their way to the kitchen. Lori was bustling around, putting away the leftover pizza and wiping the table. Her lips were creased into a frown, but there was no trace of tears on her face.

"I was going to do that when I came back in." Ava stepped closer and held out a hand for the rag.

But Lori only scrubbed harder. "I don't mind."

"Okay." Ava leaned against the counter, watching her aunt scrub at a spot that was already spotless. "You want to talk about it?"

"Nothing to talk about."

Ava rolled her eyes. "You may be the parental figure here, Aunt Lori, but that doesn't mean I can't tell when something is wrong."

Lori kept her head down, but Ava saw the drop of water that plopped onto the table.

"What is it? Did something happen to a patient?"

Lori shook her head but remained silent, still looking down. "Michael was offered a job," she said quietly. "In Omaha."

"Nebraska?" The state name popped out of Ava's mouth, even as she pictured Joseph in the sixth-grade geography bee, proudly announcing that Omaha was in Minnesota. He had been the first one out.

She pushed the memory away. Now was not the time to be thinking of Joseph—even if it seemed like every moment was a moment to be thinking of him lately.

Lori nodded miserably. "His mom lives there, and she's getting older and . . . He applied months ago. Before we were . . ."

Ava set a hand on top of Lori's to stop the scrubbing. "Is he going to take it?"

Lori sniffed. "How can he not? It's the perfect job for him. He would be so good at it, and— He asked what I thought, which was totally unfair. What was I supposed to say?"

"Well, you clearly don't want him to go."

Lori pulled her hand out from under Ava's and started scrubbing again. "That shouldn't matter. It's not like we've made each other any promises. We've only been dating for a month and a half. And the job doesn't start until next school year. I can't assume that we'll still be— That it will matter what I— I'm not going to be the one to stop him from having the life he should have."

Ava sighed. That felt painfully familiar.

And yet—

What if Aunt Lori was wrong? What if Ava had been wrong?

She thought again of the way Joseph had looked at her tonight. Thought of the eight years she'd gone without him. Thought of how it felt every time she was with him now.

"You have to tell him how you feel," Ava said finally.

"What if he goes anyway?" Lori clutched at the dishrag.

Ava sighed. "Then at least you'll know."

# Chapter 25

The workday on Monday was agonizingly long, even though Joseph had a constant stream of patients.

But all day, all he wanted to do was close the clinic, march down the street to Ava's studio, burst through the doors, and give her the longest, deepest kiss he'd ever given her.

The kiss he was still kicking himself for not giving her Saturday night.

But the same thing that had stopped him then stopped him now.

What if she didn't want that?

Even so, he had to see her again.

He'd had to go to Beautiful Savior's early service yesterday because he'd promised Asher he'd help with a fishing clinic, so he hadn't gotten to see her then, and it was driving him crazy.

Fortunately, around ten this morning, he'd come up with another brilliant plan: He'd called and asked Ava if she could take a new set of headshots for his business cards.

He'd been sure she'd say no—but she'd surprised him with a yes. And with the idea to include Tasha and Princess in them.

As the clock *finally* turned to five, he forwarded the phones to his emergency answering service, clipped a leash on each dog, and stepped outside.

He'd always thought mid-September was the perfect time of year in Tennessee, and today was no exception—warm but not too hot, sunny with a few wisps of clouds, birds singing, river gurgling, and people smiling. And his smile was probably biggest of all as he got closer to Ava's studio.

He pulled in a quick breath and opened the door.

Princess darted through instantly, yanking her leash right out of his hand. Tasha gave him a dignified look and walked through at his side.

"Oh lighten up." Joseph laughed at the Samoyed. "You were young once too."

He heard the skitter of puppy toenails on the floor in the next room, followed by a crash.

"Then again, maybe you were right." He tugged Tasha into the studio, an apology ready on his lips for whatever disaster Princess had caused. She still wasn't the most stable on her feet, though she was adjusting nicely to the slight twist in her back leg.

But he found Ava laughing as she picked up a metal washtub that had tipped over on top of Princess.

"Guess she wanted a bath." The smile Ava gave him made him wish he were the photographer. It was the same smile he'd fallen in love with all those years ago. The same smile he had wanted to kiss so badly Saturday night.

"That's not how she felt the other night when I tried to give her a bath," Joseph said. "I didn't know she could run that fast."

Ava laughed, scooping up the troublemaking puppy and nuzzling the dog's nose with her own.

After a moment, she stepped toward him and held out Princess. "If you want to hold her, I think that will work best."

Joseph took the dog, letting his fingers brush against Ava's for the merest fraction of a second.

But that was a mistake. Because it only made him want to take her hand and pull her close.

Ava pointed to a spot in front of the camera, all business now. "Right there. If you maybe kneel on one leg, with the other one up, we can put Tasha in front of you."

Joseph moved to where she'd indicated, then knelt as she'd described.

The moment he was in position, he froze. How many times had he dreamed of getting down on one knee in front of Ava? Only, in his dreams he was always holding a ring, not a puppy.

Ava turned from where she'd been adjusting a light. As soon as her eyes fell on Joseph, her mouth opened, and pink bled through the makeup on her cheeks.

"Oh. Um—" She turned to adjust the light again. "Let's try with you standing and Tasha at your feet."

Obediently, he stood, not taking his eyes from her, though she didn't look at him again until he'd gotten up off the ground.

"Okay. Um. Let's try– Uh—" She was adorable when she was flustered, and Joseph had to work to keep his grin hidden.

"What?" she demanded.

Apparently he hadn't kept it as hidden as he'd thought.

"Nothing. You're just cute when you work."

She rolled her eyes, but Joseph was pretty sure that now she was the one trying to hide a grin.

"Tasha, sit." Ava sounded more certain now, and Tasha obeyed instantly. "And Joseph, can you hold Princess in one arm and rest your other hand on Tasha's head?"

He tried diligently, but Princess was more than a little wiggly.

Ava snapped a few pictures but lowered the camera almost instantly. "This isn't working." She chewed her lip, looking around the room. "Let's try something else."

She grabbed a stool from behind her and plunked it next to him. "Sit."

Both he and Tasha obeyed.

"All right, now set Princess on your lap."

The puppy was much less wiggly like this, and Ava snapped pictures for a couple of minutes, having Joseph move his hands or his head slightly, changing where she stood, calling for the dogs' attention.

"That was better." She lowered the camera and looked at a few of the pictures. "But I really do think on your knee was best. Has more energy. Let's try it again."

She pulled the stool out of the way as Joseph carefully got down onto one knee again. This time, Ava didn't even seem to recognize the significance of the stance. She matter-of-factly placed Tasha in front of him and adjusted Princess on his knee, then started clicking away again.

"That should do it," she said way too soon.

"That's it?" He wasn't ready to say goodbye again.

"Yep." She gave him a strange look. "Unless—" She seemed to second-guess herself but then shrugged. "Unless you want some pictures of just the dogs. Might make a good replacement for those dressed-up cat pictures at the clinic."

"Yes." Joseph's reply may have been a little too enthusiastic for pet photos, but he didn't care. Anything that meant he could spend more time with Ava was a good thing.

"All right."

Was it him, or did she look pleased he'd said yes?

"Let's start with Tasha. I have a feeling Princess is going to be the more challenging one."

She wasn't wrong about that. Tasha sat perfectly for her pictures, but when they moved on to Princess, they couldn't get the puppy to stay in place long enough to get a single good shot.

"I give up," Joseph finally said, after retrieving her from under the table for the twelfth time.

"Here, how about I try?" Ava stepped toward the puppy, pulling her camera strap over her head.

"And who's going to take the picture?"

She held the camera out to him, but he shook his head. "I don't know the first thing about how to use that."

"I have everything set up for you. All you have to do is push this button." She indicated a silver circle on top of the camera. "Just make sure not to get me in the picture."

Joseph took the camera, which was much heavier than he'd expected, and lifted it tentatively to his eyes, bringing the focus to rest on the spot where Ava had managed to get Princess to sit still.

"Now," Ava called, letting go of the dog.

Joseph pressed the button—just in time for Princess to scamper off.

Ava chased after her and returned her to the spot on the floor. "Get ready." She patted Princess, holding her in place. "Set." She lifted one hand. "Go."

Joseph snapped the picture as Ava removed her other hand. The puppy sat long enough for him to get one shot, then scampered toward Ava.

"Keep shooting," Ava called. "This might be the best we can do."

Joseph kept pressing the button as the puppy licked the hand Ava had reached out to push her back into position. The dog instantly scampered toward Ava again, climbing onto her knee.

Ava's laugh was so perfect that Joseph couldn't resist.

He lifted the camera so that the focus rested on her face. And he pressed the button. Once and then again.

When Ava looked up, he pulled the camera away from his face.

"Think you got something we can use?" She was still smiling that smile.

"Yeah. I think I did." He passed the camera into her outstretched hands. "Thanks for letting me use this. It was pretty fun."

"Yeah? Let's take a look." She set the camera down on the table and picked up a tablet. "They'll be easier to see on here."

"Maybe I should get a camera. If you'll teach me how to use it." He didn't care if she could see through his blatant attempt to spend more time with her.

"Sure." But she was already focused on the pictures that had popped onto her tablet screen. "This is a good one." She angled the tablet so he could see it better—and he took the opportunity to step closer and bend his head over her shoulder.

It was one of the pictures of him on one knee with the dogs.

She kept clicking through the pictures, her finger deftly hitting the delete button on any that didn't meet her approval.

When she got to the pictures of Princess, she must have deleted at least two dozen before she came to the ones he'd taken.

"These aren't bad." She turned her head to smile at him over her shoulder, and his breath caught.

She was close enough that all he'd have to do was lower his head a little more and his lips could brush hers.

She turned back to the tablet, and he focused on pulling in a steadying breath. As much as his desire to kiss her had only grown since Saturday night, she hadn't indicated that anything had changed since then. Which meant he needed to stay on this side of the friendship line. The side where they didn't kiss.

Ava laughed as she got to the pictures of Princess licking her hand and then climbing her knee. But her laugh cut off abruptly as she clicked to the next picture—the one of her face.

Considering that Joseph hadn't had a clue what he was doing, the picture had turned out perfectly, capturing that smile he had wanted to hold onto forever.

Before he could say anything, her finger darted to the delete button.

"Ava!"

The second picture flashed onto the screen—and then was gone too.

"Why would you do that?" Joseph grabbed her elbow and spun her toward him.

But she jerked out of his grasp and took a step backwards. "I told you not to take a picture of me."

The tablet shook in her hands, and he could see the tears gathering behind her eyelids.

Oh man. Had he messed everything up?

He took a slow step toward her and eased the tablet from her, setting it on the table.

She covered her face with her hands, but gently, he pulled them away and wrapped his own hands around them.

She refused to look at him, but that was okay.

"I don't think you realize how beautiful you are, Ava. You're strong, you're caring, you're compassionate, you're funny, you're—"

"Yeah," she cut him off. "I get it. Beauty is more than skin deep. But, Joseph, I used to be—" She gave him a helpless look. "I was supposed to be a model."

Joseph tightened his hands around hers. "Beauty *is* more than skin deep, Ava. Your beauty is so deep. But when I say you're beautiful, I mean everything. Including this." He touched a hand to her face, letting his fingers graze the scars.

"Don't say that." A tear splattered onto her cheek, right above his hand, and he slid his thumb to wipe it away.

"Why not?" Gently, he rubbed his fingers across her scars.

She shook her head, two more tears falling.

He wiped them away too.

"I'm not that girl anymore, Joseph. I'm not beautiful. Look at me."

"I *am* looking at you." He brought his other hand to her other cheek. "And you are beautiful."

"Joseph, please—"

"I'll keep saying it until you believe it, Ava. You're beautiful." He let his head tilt closer to hers. "You're beautiful."

Her long exhale breezed over his lips.

Another few centimeters and—

Joseph let go of her and stepped back, clearing his throat. He'd gotten too close to the line. "I'm sorry. I should go."

Ava's eyes opened wide in confusion and—was that anger he saw there?

"If I'm so beautiful—" She jabbed a finger at his chest. "Why can't you bring yourself to kiss me? You can talk sweet all you want, but when it comes down to it, I repulse you." She gave an angry swipe at the tears still on her cheeks.

Joseph ran both hands over his head and gave a disbelieving laugh. "I'm the furthest thing from repulsed by you, Ava. I am so—You are so—" His breath came in gasps as he fought to keep from striding over there and proving to her right now just how badly he wanted to kiss her. "But I don't know if *you* want to. And I promised you I wouldn't ask you for more than friendship, so—" He held up his hands, working to gentle his voice. "This is me not asking. If you've changed your mind"—*Please, Lord, let her have changed her mind*—"you have to let me know. I can be over there and kissing you in half a second flat." He grinned, trying to diffuse the intensity he was feeling right now.

Ava blinked at him, running her fingers back and forth over the scars on her lip. "I don't know," she finally whispered. "I . . ." She shook her head, as if she was at a loss for words.

"It's okay," he said quietly. He called for Tasha and Princess, and the dogs bounded over. "Take as much time as you need."

He reached for the door. "I'm not going anywhere."

# Chapter 26

If he could, Joseph would go back in time and kick himself.

What had he been thinking, telling Ava to take as much time as she needed? It had only been three days, and he was already going out of his mind.

He'd counted on work to provide a good distraction, but even that wasn't proving to be much help.

He escorted Mr. Glover and his aged pit bull to the waiting room, careful to keep a smile on his face until they'd left. Then he sagged against the counter, rubbing his hands over his cheeks. At least he only had four more appointments today.

"You look like you could use a pick-me-up."

Joseph jumped at the voice. He wasn't used to having an assistant here with him yet.

"I'm fine."

"I know what you need." Madison slid her rolling chair across the floor behind the desk so that she was directly in front of him.

Yeah. So did he. He needed Ava.

"Pie," Madison said, triumph ringing from her voice. "How about I run out and get you a slice?"

Joseph considered. Pie did sound good. And if Madison went to get it, he'd have a few moments to himself. Not that working with Madison was all bad. Though he'd certainly had his doubts when he'd hired her earlier this week, he hadn't had much choice, given that of the three applicants, she was the only one even remotely proficient with a computer. Already, Madison had completely computerized the appointment system, and she was in the process of sorting through all of Dr. Gallagher's antiquated records. Even so, Joseph missed the peace and quiet of having the office to himself.

At least while Madison was out getting the pie, he could call Ava.

*No. No calling Ava.* He'd told her he'd give her time, and that was what he was going to do.

"I'll be back in a flash." Madison grabbed her purse and headed for the door.

Joseph made a mental note to pay her back when she returned.

Then he pulled out his phone and stared at it. Still nothing from Ava.

Maybe it wouldn't hurt to send one little text, just so she'd know he was thinking of her.

He moved his finger toward the screen.

Then he pulled it back and tucked the phone into his pocket.

If he sent that text and she didn't respond, that would be worse than not sending it at all.

At least this way he could tell himself there was still hope.

It had taken Ava three days. But she'd finally worked up the courage.

She was going to tell Joseph that she *had* changed her mind. She *did* want to be with him.

And she was going to sweeten the deal with pie.

She hadn't been able to stop thinking about those almost kisses all week. And every time she did, all she could think was what a fool she'd been not to realize how badly she'd wanted them.

She locked the door to her studio, where she'd just finished taking pictures of a sweet six-month-old girl, then set off on the short walk to

Daisy's. With the beautiful fall weather, the streets were busier than usual, and she ducked her head, letting her hair form a protective barrier around her face as she walked.

She didn't look up until she was nearly to Daisy's—and when she did, she drew to a stop.

Even though it was two in the afternoon on a Thursday, the parking lot was packed.

She couldn't go in there—not alone, not with all those people.

Could she?

She clenched her hands into fists, taking a few deep breaths and picturing the look of delight Joseph would wear when she passed him the unexpected treat.

Maybe she could do this after all.

Tucking her head down again but making her steps purposeful, she marched for the restaurant's door. Her heart battered against her ribs like she was marching into battle instead of into a pie shop, but she made it through the door and to the back of the line.

As she waited, she pulled out her phone, pretending to check it as an excuse not to look up.

Although the shop was loud with voices and laughter and clanking dishes, Ava couldn't help but overhear the conversation taking place in front of her.

"I heard you got a job," a woman's voice was saying. "I almost didn't believe it."

"I thought it was time." This voice sounded familiar to Ava, but she couldn't quite place it. She allowed herself a quick peek up through her hair.

It was Madison, standing at the counter to place her order but facing backwards to talk to the woman behind her in line.

Ava ducked her head again. Running into Madison in the parking lot at Murf's a few weeks back had been enough. She wasn't in the mood for another awkward conversation.

"I bet you did." The other woman giggled. "The pie's a nice touch. Fastest way to a man's heart . . ."

"That's not what this is," Madison said. Her stylish boots shuffled to the side as the line moved forward. "He's just having a rough day."

"Ah, a rough day. Good thing you're there to comfort him."

"Stop it." Madison's voice held a laugh. "This really *is* only about the job."

"Whatever you say." The other woman made a dismissive sound.

Madison said something Ava didn't catch, and then her boots disappeared out the door.

Ava shuffled forward with the rest of the line, a feeling of unease hovering over her that went beyond nerves over what she was about to tell Joseph.

"Can I help you?" The woman at the counter waved her forward a few moments later.

It wasn't too late to back out. She could leave. Forget her whole plan.

But she made herself place the order. "One slice of blueberry and one lemon. To go." She could always give the lemon to Aunt Lori if she couldn't bring herself to finish the journey to Joseph's office.

The woman rang up the order, her eyes straying to Ava's face only once before darting away. Ava made herself hold her ground.

"Here you go." The cashier passed Ava a bag with her boxed-up pie slices.

"Thank you." Ava pretended not to notice as the woman allowed herself a longer stare.

Outside, she forced herself to direct her footsteps toward River Falls Veterinary. As the afternoon sun warmed her, she dared to lift her head a little bit.

Her eyes fell on the river, sliding lazily along its banks. She smiled at it—maybe if Joseph wasn't busy, they could take a walk after their pie.

When she got to the veterinary office, she was relieved to find the parking lot nearly empty. She hadn't considered what she'd do if he was with a patient. Wait, she supposed. She had the rest of the day free, and this was too important to put off any longer.

Gulping in a deep breath to fortify herself, she pulled the door open.

The front lobby area was empty, but the click of puppy toes clattered toward her. Tasha scrabbled to her first, giving her a happy sniff, followed by Princess, who appeared to have doubled in size yet again.

Ava bent to pet the puppy, whose whole body wagged in excitement. "How's my girl?" She hadn't meant to start thinking of the puppy as hers—but apparently somewhere along the line she had.

"You two running the place today?" She stood and made her way through the lobby and down the hallway toward Joseph's office, a current of nervous energy propelling her limbs.

The door was open, so she didn't knock. "Surprise. I brought—"

She froze.

Joseph was leaning against the edge of his desk, laughing, holding a half-eaten piece of pie.

On the couch across the room, Madison was laughing and eating pie too.

"Ava." Joseph jumped up from the desk, coming toward her. His smile was as big and warm as ever, but Ava wondered if she detected a trace of guilt under it. "What are you doing here?"

"I was just— I mean— I should go. You two are in the middle of something."

"Don't be silly." Joseph took the bag out of her hands. "You can't say surprise and then take it back."

"I should get back to the front desk." Madison stood, sending Ava a look that screamed guilty as she hurried out of the room, dropping the rest of her pie in the trash on the way.

"Pie." Joseph laughed as he peered into the bag from Ava. "Two slices in fifteen minutes. Must be my lucky day."

Ava swallowed. Two equally delicious slices of pie. Two very unequally matched women. It wasn't hard to guess which he would choose. Just like he had for prom.

*That's not fair*, she reminded herself.

Joseph hadn't had a choice for prom—not really. She'd made that choice for him when she broke up with him.

"What was Madison . . ." She bit her tongue. It was none of her business.

Joseph pulled out the pie slices and passed the blueberry one to her. "Oh, I hired her as my new assistant. She started Tuesday, and she's a miracle worker. The way she's organized everything already."

Tuesday. That explained why Ava hadn't heard anything from Joseph since then.

"I'm really glad you stopped by." Joseph took a step closer to her.

She opened her pie, letting the clamshell packaging serve as a flimsy shield.

But Joseph didn't stop. "I've been wanting to—"

There was a knock on the doorframe. "Sorry, Dr. Calvano." Madison sounded ridiculously formal. "Mrs. Sampson is here with Chester. Did you want me to tell them to wait or . . ."

"I have to go anyway." Ava closed up the pie she hadn't yet taken a bite of. "I just wanted to drop off the pie and tell you . . ." She scrambled for something to say. "Congratulations on your first therapy dog visit." Yes. That worked.

She turned toward the door.

"Wait," Joseph called after her. "Will you be around later? Maybe we could—"

"Sorry, I have plans." Ava's voice was flat.

He'd know it was a lie, of course. She never had plans.

But it was the best she could come up with right now.

# Chapter 27

"Good sermon today, Dad." Joseph held out a hand to shake his father's as he filed out of the church.

It truly had been, even if Joseph had struggled to focus, his thoughts constantly drifting to the person who wasn't sitting next to him this week.

When Ava had shown up at his office unexpectedly the other day—and with his favorite pie—he'd made the mistake of letting himself hope, however briefly, that she'd made up her mind, that she did want to be with him.

But that hope had dried up the moment she made her escape—and he wasn't sure if he could handle resurrecting it.

He'd tried texting her, asking if everything was all right, inviting her to church—but all had gone unread.

"You all right?" Dad gave him that compassionate look that made him so good at getting people to share their burdens with him.

"Yeah. I guess."

"Why don't you come by for lunch?" Dad clapped a hand to his shoulder. "Invite Ava if you want."

He did want to. But he wasn't sure he could take one more unanswered message from her.

Maybe he had to face the fact that he and Ava were never going to happen.

He moved out of the way of the people behind him. "I'll pick up the hot chicken."

Half an hour later, the smell of hot chicken filling the car and making him practically drool, Joseph pulled into Dad's driveway. He grabbed the chicken off the seat, thankful he'd left the dogs home. Otherwise, he'd have spent the whole drive restraining them from the food.

Instead of thinking of Ava.

On second thought, maybe he should have brought the dogs.

He let himself into the house and headed straight for the kitchen.

Dad already had the table set. For three.

"No Ava?"

Joseph plunked the chicken on the table and dropped into a chair, leaning his head back to stare at the ceiling. "Nope."

"Something happen with you two?"

Joseph could hear Dad's real question: Did you do something to screw this up?

Joseph shook his head. "I honestly don't know. One moment I could swear she feels the same way I do. And the next—I don't know. It's like she's scared, like she doesn't think I could possibly love her."

"And do you? Love her?"

"Of course I do."

"How much?" Dad's eyes pierced Joseph's.

"What do you mean, how much?" How did you put a quantity on love?

"I mean, do you love her more than you love yourself?"

Joseph didn't have to think about it. "Yes."

"Do you love her enough to let her go, if that's what she wants?"

"You don't think she wants to be with me?"

"That's not what I'm saying." Dad stabbed a piece of chicken and set it on his plate. "I'm just saying, are you willing to do whatever she needs? Even at your own expense?"

Joseph hesitated. But he'd rather hurt himself a thousand times than see Ava get hurt once.

"Yes," he said. "I'm willing."

"Good." Dad folded his hands. "Should we pray then?"

Joseph nodded, closing his eyes as Dad started the prayer. "Father in Heaven, you are the source of all love. As we show love for others, help us to always keep your love first in our hearts. Help Joseph to continue to show love for Ava, in whatever way she needs. In Jesus' name. Amen."

"Amen." Joseph sat back, staring at his plate. He couldn't believe he might really have to give Ava up. But if that was what she needed, it was what he'd do.

"Don't look so downhearted, son." Dad passed the chicken. "I wouldn't give up hope just yet."

"But you just said—"

"I said, *if* it's what she needs." He took a bite of chicken. "But I wouldn't be so sure it is."

"How am I supposed to know?" Could this whole thing get any more confusing?

"Wait. Give her time. Be—"

"Patient, yeah." Joseph jammed his fingers into his hair. "It's hard."

Dad's laugh boomed around the room, and Joseph stared at him. "Glad you find this amusing."

"Sorry." But Dad was still chuckling. "Do you know how long I had to wait for your mother to agree to go out with me?"

Joseph lifted his eyes to Dad's face. His father had never shied away from talking about Mama since her death, but he rarely mentioned their younger years. "I don't know—five minutes?"

His parents had been the type of couple who rarely spent time apart. Mama often helped Dad in his ministry, and Dad made time to go to the grocery store with her every week.

Dad guffawed harder. “Two years. It took me two years of asking and giving her space. Of showing her I was a friend and she could trust me. Of waiting.”

“Didn’t you go crazy?” He’d already waited eight years. Two more might kill him.

“Oh yeah.” Dad shook his head. “But it was worth it.”

Joseph believed that. He knew it would all be worth it if Ava said yes in the end. But— “What if she had said no?”

Dad sobered. “Do you believe God works all things to the good of those who love him?”

Joseph nodded.

“Well then. You just answered your own question. But I wouldn’t be too worried about that.”

“What does that mean?”

“It means—” Dad grinned at him. “I’ve seen the way Ava looks at you.”

# Chapter 28

Ava tucked Joseph's photos into an envelope. She sealed it, then stared at it. Should she walk it over to his office or drop it in the mail?

The thought of seeing him right now left her stomach in all kinds of tangles. Not to mention, if she went over there, it wasn't only Joseph she'd see. Madison would be there too.

She'd tried hard all week to scrub the image of Joseph and Madison laughing together in his office from her brain. But instead, it had morphed into an image of them eating dinner together, raising children together, *belonging* together.

It wasn't jealousy.

That wasn't what she felt.

It was certainty.

Certainty that Madison was the kind of woman Joseph should be with. They *looked* right together. They made the perfect picture.

She let out a long, slow breath and addressed the envelope.

Someday he'd thank her.

She slid her chair back. She'd drop this at the post office on her way home.

But just as she stood, the studio door opened. Ava looked up, annoyed to have her mission interrupted.

She fell back into her chair with an audible thud as Madison marched inside.

Ava may not be jealous of Madison. But that didn't mean she necessarily wanted to chat with her.

Madison hurried toward her. "Ava, I'm glad I caught you."

Ava's stomach clenched at Madison's perfectly made up face. Not a single blemish marred its smooth surface, and yet it wasn't overdone. She was a natural beauty.

Like Ava had been once.

Ava rubbed her cheek. "What can I do for you?"

"Nothing really." Madison picked up a pen from the cup Ava kept on the edge of her desk, twirling it in her fingers.

"Okay, then . . ." Would it be rude to point out that it was past closing time?

"I stopped by because I wanted to get something straight."

Ava closed her eyes.

Here it came.

Madison was going to say she liked Joseph. And Ava was going to have to pretend she was fine with it. No—not pretend. She *was* fine with it.

"Look, Madison, if this is about Joseph—"

"Of course it's about Joseph." Madison gave her a disbelieving look, as if it couldn't possibly be about anything else.

"You can save your breath. There's nothing going on between us. So you're free to . . ." She made a vague gesture, hoping Madison could fill in the rest.

But Madison crossed her arms, towering over Ava. "That's what you think? That I want to date Joseph?"

Ava held back a snort. Madison had never been a good actress. "I heard you in the pie shop the other day. I know you started working for Joseph because you like him." She held up a hand as Madison tried to interrupt. "No, it's fine. Really. You and Joseph make much more sense than he and I do."

Understanding dawned on Madison's face. "You overheard Mindy. She was being stupid when she said that. I took the job with Joseph because I wanted my family to see— Well, never mind. But it had nothing to do with Joseph. I mean, yeah, sure, maybe the thought of dating him crossed my mind for thirty seconds. Which is how long it took me to realize he was still in love with you."

Ava shook her head. She knew he thought he was—but that was only because he thought she was still Old Ava—beautiful, happy, high school Ava—not New Ava. Not broken Ava.

"Ava—" Madison dropped the pen back into the cup and leaned forward against the desk. "The man does not stop talking about you. All. Day. Long. He's driving me a little bit crazy if you want to know the truth." She gave a half-laugh as she pushed off the desk. "So what I don't understand is why you keep pushing him away."

"I'm not—"

Madison gave her a hard look and crossed her arms. "Trust me, Ava. I know a thing or two about pushing people away, and that's exactly what you're doing. You need to either go all in with him or let him go. If I were you, I know which I'd choose."

Madison spun on her heel and stalked toward the door.

Ava stared after her, speechless, then dropped her head into her hands and rubbed at her temples.

Madison was . . . right.

It was time for her to make a choice.

# Chapter 29

Joseph blinked at the text from Ava that had just popped onto his screen.

*Can we talk?*

His stomach tightened. This could be really, really good or really, really bad. Everything he'd been praying for—or an end to all his hopes.

*Of course. Name the time and place.* His fingers tapped out the reply quickly.

*Now? Your place?*

Before he could reply that, yes, that would be perfect, there was a knock on the door.

He glared at it. Now was not the time for an unexpected visitor. Whatever unsolicited salesman was there, he hoped they were ready to be dismissed quickly.

But when he pulled the door open, his breath left him in a hard rush. The dogs greeted her before he could, and she bent to give them each a pat.

"Ava." He finally found his voice, though it came out strangely gruff.

She didn't seem to notice. "You really want this?" She shifted from side to side, her fingers wrapping themselves in Tasha's fur.

A seedling of hope sprang up in his heart.

He tried his hardest to keep it from roaring to full life. “Could you be more specific? By ‘this,’ you mean . . .”

“Me. Are you sure you want me?” Ava lifted her eyes to his, and there was no holding it back any longer.

That hope in his chest burst into full bloom in the time it took him to step forward and pull her to him. “More than anything.”

Her arms wrapped around him in return, and he let himself breathe in the jasmine scent that he associated with his happiest memories.

He was afraid to loosen his grip, in case she changed her mind, but both Tasha and Princess attempted to wriggle between them.

Reluctantly, he let go and stepped back. His arms instantly protested, but he resisted gathering her to him again. He didn’t know how fast or slow she wanted to take things.

“Do you want to come in or . . .” He’d spent so much time praying that she’d change her mind about dating him that he hadn’t planned for what would happen if she did.

“I’d like that.” Her smile reflected the same joy he felt pulsing through his own veins.

He led her to the kitchen. “How about something to drink?” So far so good. He’d take this one step at a time; after he got her something to drink, he’d figure out what came next. And then what came after that.

“Water is great, thanks.” Ava leaned against the countertop that was currently strewn with papers he was in the midst of sorting.

He grabbed a glass and moved to the fridge to fill it. “Sorry about the mess. I was cleaning out some old files.”

Ava shrugged. “Seriously, Joseph, you’ve seen my storage room so you know– What’s this?”

Paper rustled, and Joseph froze.

He knew before he turned around what she had found.

“That’s . . .”

But she was already peering at it. “Dear Ava.” She looked up.

“I wrote to you,” he said quietly, setting the water in front of her.

She didn’t seem to notice. “When?”

He glanced at the date at the top of the page. “That one was from right after the fire. Some were from the years after that.” Right up until now. But fortunately the most recent one was still in his bedroom.

She glanced up at him. “You never sent them.”

He shook his head. “I didn’t think you’d want to read them.” He shoved his hands in his pockets. “I was afraid they’d only hurt you more.” Or maybe he’d been afraid that not getting an answer from her would only hurt *him* more.

She pressed her lips together as she continued to read.

“You can have them,” he said suddenly. “All of them.” He strode toward his bedroom, returning a second later with the letter he’d written last night.

She gave him a quizzical look. “Why wasn’t this one with the others?”

He shrugged. “It’s the newest one. I just wrote it. Last night.”

“Will you read it to me?”

He nodded, even as a wave of uncertainty washed over him.

The things he’d said in this letter—what if they ruined everything?

# Chapter 30

Ava settled next to Joseph on his sofa, letting her shoulder brush lightly against his. The dogs plopped on the floor at their feet.

Joseph looked at her with a nervous smile, then wrapped an arm around her. She sighed as she nestled against his side and rested her head on his shoulder. How had she forgotten how perfectly she fit here?

"You're sure you want me to read this?" Joseph kissed the top of her head as he unfolded the paper.

"I'm sure." What she'd read of the other letter had made her heart ache for the love she'd pushed away.

But that had been eight years ago. She wanted to know how he felt now.

"Dear Ava." Joseph's voice was tender as he read his own handwriting, and Ava closed her eyes so she wouldn't be tempted to read ahead.

"I'm writing this because there's something I have to say to you, and I'm not sure I have the courage to say it in person."

She heard him swallow, and she snuggled closer, letting the feel of his hand on her arm send warm tingles up her back. She was pretty sure she would never want to leave this spot.

"And that is," Joseph continued, "that I promised you I wouldn't pursue a relationship with you. But I haven't been one hundred percent faithful to that promise, at least not in my heart. I've looked for ways to spend time with you, to convince you that you and me together is best for us both. I've even prayed for that. But maybe it's not fair for me to try to change your mind. Maybe what I need to do is just be a friend to you. The way you asked."

Ava wiggled out of her cozy spot in his arms. Now that she'd said yes, was he saying he didn't want this after all?

But he cinched her to him. "Just listen," he whispered, then turned back to the paper. "As much as I want to be with you—and believe me, that's a lot—even more than that, I want you to be happy. To have everything you need. And if I'm not the one who can bring you that happiness, if I'm not the one you need, then I'm not the one you should be with."

Ava tried again to sit up. She had to tell him—he *was* the one who made her happy. The one she needed. He always had been.

But his arm anchored her in place.

"So simply say the word, and I will stop looking for more," he read. "But before you decide, I want you to know one thing—no matter what, I will always be here for you. As a friend. Or as more. Because I love you, Ava." He turned her slightly in his arms so he could look at her. "I will always love you."

He set the paper down and took her hands. "Now I have to ask you something."

She nodded, not quite able to speak, her heart full to the bursting point. She didn't want him to give her up. Not even close. But knowing that he was willing to, if that was what she wanted . . .

"Are you sure *you* want this?" Joseph tucked a piece of hair behind her ear, studying her closely.

She nodded, still unable to find the words to reply to that beautiful letter.

"Good." Joseph's hands came to her face. "Then, if you don't mind, there's something I've been wanting to do for ages."

His lips caught hers, and she was swept away in his kiss.

It was strong and tender and just as sweet as she'd remembered, only with a depth to it she'd never felt before.

When they pulled apart, he rested his forehead on hers.

"That was . . ." But words were too small for what that was.

"It was." Joseph caressed her cheek.

"And you didn't mind . . ." She touched a hand to the roughened part of her lips.

He leaned closer and caught her lips in another kiss. When he straightened, he grinned at her. "Does that answer your question?"

"I think so." Ava grabbed his hands and tugged him closer again. "But maybe we should try one more time. Just to be sure."

"As many times as it takes." His arms wrapped around her, his hands coming to rest on the small of her back, as he kissed her with a strength that stole her breath.

When they finally separated, he just looked at her. "Now what?"

She loved being close enough to feel his breath whisper over her lips.

"Now—" She tilted her head to kiss him again. "Now I suppose you should ask me out."

# Chapter 31

"You're absolutely sure this is a good idea?" Zeb drummed his fingers on the hood of his police cruiser. He'd been making a round of the neighborhood when he'd spotted Joseph outside with the dogs—so he said. But Joseph got the distinct impression that his brother had been checking up on him.

It was Joseph's own fault. He'd been so excited when Ava had said yes last night that he'd texted his siblings to ask where he should take her. Simeon, Grace, Benjamin, and Asher had all weighed in—he was taking Simeon's suggestion to take her to the Depot, an old train depot on the river that had been converted into a steak house—but Zeb hadn't responded.

Joseph should have known that his brother wasn't going to remain silent.

"Yeah, Zeb. It's the best idea I've ever had." He grinned. Eight years of hope were about to come true. Even his brother's cross-examination wasn't going to ruin his exuberant mood.

"And if things don't work out? Again?" Zeb crossed his arms in front of him, leaning against his car.

"They will." Joseph was beyond positive of that. He wasn't going to do anything to ruin this second chance.

"Joseph." Zeb's voice carried the same warning it had the time he'd pulled Joseph over. "You have to be realistic. You can't guarantee that."

"Nice sentiment, Zeb. Maybe you should say that to your wife," Joseph said dryly. Honestly, Zeb of all people should understand, given that he and Carly had been together since they were like thirteen.

Zeb straightened. "I hope it works out, Joseph. I really do. I just don't want you to be surprised if it doesn't. I've gotta run. Let me know how it goes."

"Yeah." Joseph shook his head. He knew Zeb was just being the protective one, as always. But for once, it would be nice if he recognized that Joseph was old enough not to need protecting anymore.

"Perfect. That's how it's going to go—absolutely perfect," he muttered to the dogs as Zeb's car drove away. He shook off the doubts Zeb's comments had nearly conjured up. Things were going to be just as perfect as they'd always been between him and Ava. He had no doubts.

Ava paced back and forth in front of the window, alternately staring at the driveway and gulping in strangled breaths. What had she been thinking, saying she'd go out with Joseph? Half a dozen times today, she'd considered calling and canceling. But every time she'd gotten her phone out, she'd pictured the disappointment she'd hear in his voice, pictured the way her own heart would scold her, and she'd put the phone away.

She glanced across the room into the mirror that hung near the door. Her ankle-length floral skirt and long-sleeved shirt weren't going to make any fashion magazines—but at least they covered her scars. She wished her makeup job had turned out better—her hand had been a little shaky when she'd applied it—but there was nothing she could do about it now. Joseph would be here any minute.

Oh, why hadn't she just canceled?

Griffin rubbed up against her leg, and Ava stopped her pacing to pet him. "You be a good boy. Aunt Lori should be home a little later." Her aunt had been spending longer and longer hours at work lately, and Michael hadn't been over for dinner once since Lori had found out about his job offer. Ava had tried to talk to her aunt about it, but Lori kept pushing her questions off.

Griffin let out a short bark and trotted to the window. Ava's heart shot up to her throat and ricocheted around for a few seconds before finally resuming its spot in her chest.

She pulled in a shaky breath. "I guess this is it." Her stomach still swirling, she made herself open the front door, finding Joseph halfway up the steps. He quickly stashed his arm behind his back.

"You know I saw that, right?" She laughed even as her breath caught at the realization that he'd brought her flowers.

"What these?" Joseph pulled a stunning bouquet of roses and lilies from behind his back. "These are for Griffin."

At the sound of his name, Griffin charged outside and probably would have devoured the whole bouquet if Joseph hadn't deftly tossed it over the dog's head to Ava. Instinctively, she put her hands out to catch it.

"Nice one." Joseph reached into the pocket of his gray dress pants and pulled out a treat. "Here, Griffin." He showed it to the dog and then tossed it to the far side of the driveway.

As Griffin took off after it, Joseph closed the distance between them and wrapped her in his arms. She let his lemongrass scent envelop her as she brought her arms around his back and lifted her face to his. Maybe this wasn't such a terrible idea after all.

Too soon, Griffin was wedging his head between them, sniffing at Joseph's pocket for another treat.

"Sorry, boy, that was the only one." Joseph pulled back from Ava but slid his hand down her arm and wrapped her fingers in his. "You look beautiful."

Ava opened her mouth to protest, but Joseph silenced her with another kiss.

"Should we go?" he asked as he straightened.

Ava was too breathless to do more than nod. She brought Griffin inside, put the flowers in a vase, and followed Joseph out to his car, waiting as he opened the passenger door for her. Before she could slide inside, he stopped her with another kiss.

"Tonight is going to be perfect." He squeezed her hand as he gestured for her to get in the car. "Just like it used to be."

Ava nodded and got into the car.

"Remember our first date?" Joseph asked as he pulled out of the driveway a moment later. "I was so nervous I thought I was going to throw up on you."

Ava laughed with him—but an uneasiness started to build in her chest. It only grew stronger as dusk fell and they got closer to River Falls and he continued to talk about their previous dates—their previous life.

That was what he wanted, she realized suddenly. That old life back.

Well, so did she.

But the difference was that she knew she wasn't capable of giving that to him. She was too different from the girl she'd once been.

"You okay?" Joseph asked as he parked the car in front of the Depot. "You seem really quiet tonight."

Ava forced a smile. "I'm good. Just listening to you."

Joseph's laugh was warm and unforced. "Sorry. You know how I talk when I'm excited. You can do all the talking at dinner. I promise." He opened his car door, then came around to open hers.

His hand on the small of her back anchored her as they walked inside, and Ava relaxed. It was going to be fine.

It was going to be perfect, just like Joseph had said.

"Calvano. Reservation for two," Joseph said to the hostess, who smiled at him, then looked to Ava—and immediately averted her gaze.

Ava swallowed. *It was going to be perfect.*

But as the hostess led them past table after table of smiling, perfect couples, Ava could feel the eyes of everyone in the room on her. Could feel them asking why a handsome, successful, eligible man like Joseph Calvano would be with her. Could feel them . . .

Her breath jammed against her ribs, and the room spun.

She whirled, crashing right into Joseph's chest.

"Whoa. Ava." His hands came to her arms, but she shrugged out of his grip and dodged past him with a muttered, "I'm sorry, I can't," that she had no way of knowing if he heard.

She darted between the tables, muttering another apology as she almost knocked a server down. When she reached the hostess stand, she made a final mad sprint for the door.

Outside, she swiveled her head.

Now where did she go?

# Chapter 32

"Ava!" Joseph didn't care how many people in the restaurant were staring as he tore past the tables and followed her.

She had a lead on him, since it had taken him a good ten seconds to figure out what she was doing. Though he still couldn't say he knew exactly. He only knew that he had to catch up with her.

"Ava." He pushed out the door, then stopped abruptly as he spotted her sitting on the curb right in front of him.

He slowed his steps, but she didn't look up.

"Hey." He lowered himself to sit next to her. "What's up?"

She laughed softly, no humor in it. "Sorry. That must have been really embarrassing."

Joseph wrapped an arm around her shoulders, but she stiffened, and he pulled back. What had happened between the kisses they'd shared half an hour ago and now? "I'm not embarrassed, Ava. I'm worried about you. I want to help."

She glanced at him, her eyes full. "Then take me home."

"I– What?" Joseph's heart dropped right down into his stomach.

"This was a mistake, Joseph." A tear dropped onto her cheek, and she wiped it away before he could.

"What was a mistake?" he asked hoarsely. "Coming here? Or . . . ?" He couldn't bring himself to ask the rest of it. Did she think being with him was a mistake?

"I don't know," Ava whispered after a moment.

A couple approached them from across the parking lot, and Ava turned her head, shielding the left side of her face from their view. "Can we just go?"

Understanding slammed into Joseph, along with an unexplainable anger. "Why does it matter so much to you?"

Ava lifted her head, clearly shocked and confused.

"Why are your scars such a big deal to you? They don't bother anyone else."

"They're not on anyone else's face, Joseph." Heat sizzled from Ava's words, and she jumped to her feet, striding toward his car. But he propelled himself after her, grabbing her arm.

"Ava, wait." He gentled his tone. "All I'm saying is, you're beautiful. I've told you that so many times. I don't understand why you can't just believe me."

Her tears were falling freely now, and he longed to shelter her in his arms. But she remained stiff and distant.

"I don't know. I just can't . . ." Defeat hung on her words, and she slipped out of his grip, continuing more slowly toward the car.

He watched her a moment, then silently unlocked it and opened her door. His heart felt too heavy for his chest as he slid behind the wheel.

"All I'm saying," he said quietly as he started the car. "Is the Ava I knew wouldn't let something like this stop her."

He wouldn't let himself look at her. But he could feel the ache of her sigh right down to his own soul.

"That's what I've been trying to tell you," she said finally. "I'm not the same Ava you used to know."

Joseph opened his mouth to argue.

But he couldn't.

They rode the rest of the way to her house in silence.

When they arrived, he walked her to the door, praying for a way to salvage the night. "Ava—"

But she shook her head and opened the door. “Please don’t, Joseph.” And then she closed it, leaving him alone in the dark.

# Chapter 33

"Not getting dressed today?" Lori stepped onto the deck, where Ava had been curled up since before daybreak. She shrugged, checking out the rumpled pajamas she'd spent the entire day in yesterday. It wasn't like anyone was going to see her.

"So I take it you're not planning on going to church either?" Aunt Lori passed her a mug of coffee.

Ava shook her head. If she went to church, she might see Joseph. If she saw Joseph, she might wish . . .

But there was nothing to wish for.

What was done was done.

Friday night had only confirmed what she'd already suspected—that Joseph was looking for a relationship with the person she used to be, not the one she was now. And who could blame him? Frankly, she liked the old her better too. But there was no going back.

"So you're going to return to being a hermit? Because I gotta tell you, it didn't suit you."

"I was never a hermit." Hermits were creepy old guys who lived in the woods and never came out. She was a young woman who lived in the woods and never . . .

Okay, fine, she'd been a hermit. But what was so terrible about that?

"I don't see why it matters to you." Ava wrapped her hands around her mug to warm them. "You were the one who didn't want me to go out with Joseph in the first place."

"No." Lori sipped her coffee. "I didn't want you to get hurt."

Ava gestured to her pajamas, her ratty hair, her tear-tightened cheeks. "You win. You were right."

Lori sighed and set her mug on the table, pulling out a chair across from Ava. "No, I wasn't. I think maybe, sometimes, you have to take a little bit of a risk. Put yourself out there, you know?"

Ava shrugged. She was pretty sure she'd had enough of putting herself out there for a while.

"Come on." Lori clapped her hands. "Go get ready. We're going to church."

Ava choked on the swallow of coffee in her mouth. Had her aunt said *we*?

Lori made a face at her. "Don't make such a big deal out of it. I just want to get you out of the house."

Ava blinked at her aunt. She wanted to say no, to crawl back into bed and not come out . . . ever. But she might never get a chance to bring Lori to church again.

She pushed her chair back. "Give me five minutes to shower."

Ava tore through her shower at record speed, then threw on an old sweater and a pair of leggings. She eyed the makeup on the bathroom counter, then checked the time. They would be late if she took the time to do her full regimen. But she couldn't go to church with her face like this. Not when Joseph and his family and half the town of River Falls would be there.

Lori tapped on the bathroom door. "You ready?"

"Yep." She rummaged in the linen closet, pulling a makeup bag from under a stack of towels, then swept everything into it. A moving car wasn't the ideal place to do her makeup. But it was better than not doing it at all.

"You're driving," she told Lori as she emerged from the bathroom.

Lori followed her down the hall and out the door, not saying anything until they were on the road and Ava had started to apply her makeup. Fortunately, Ava had had enough practice by now that the bumps didn't throw her off too badly.

"So, you want to talk about it?" Lori slowed for one of the switchbacks coming down from the ridge.

"Talk about what?"

Lori accelerated out of the curve. "Has playing dumb ever gotten you anywhere with me?"

Ava shrugged. "We went to dinner. I realized he wants someone I'm not anymore. We came home. End of story."

"Ava, don't you think—"

"No, I don't. How are things with Mr. Germain? Has he decided about the job?"

Lori's eyes slid to her. "That was a nasty way to change the subject."

Ava dropped her hand from smoothing her concealer. "You're right. I'm sorry." That had been uncalled for. Just because she was hurting didn't mean she needed to make her aunt hurt too.

"But to answer your question, I don't think he's decided yet."

"You don't think?" Ava turned to face her aunt. "Wouldn't you be the first to know?"

Lori avoided Ava's gaze. "I haven't seen him in a couple weeks. I've been busy, and he's been . . ."

"Liar." Ava shook her head and opened her foundation, blotting it onto her face.

"Excuse me?" Lori slowed for a stop sign.

"Well." Ava pursed her lips so she could blend around them. "Here you are lecturing me about putting myself out there, and what are you doing? Hiding."

"I'm not hiding." Lori pressed her foot to the gas. "I'm giving him space to figure things out."

Ava snorted. "And does he want space?"

Lori's silence answered for her. Ava was going to push it further but decided to drop it before her aunt used her own arguments against her.

And before her heart did too.

It took all of Joseph's willpower not to turn around in the middle of the church service and look up into the balcony. When he'd seen Ava walk in with her aunt Lori, he'd nearly left poor old Mrs. Talbot, whom he'd been helping to her seat, to totter for herself. Fortunately, the old woman's grip on his arm had been strong. Unfortunately, by the time he'd gotten her seated, Ava had disappeared—to the balcony, he assumed. He'd been two steps away from running up there to apologize for Friday night when Mr. Siebert had caught him with a question about his pet Gila monster. By the time Joseph had extricated himself from that conversation, the bell had been ringing to start the service. He'd stood, undecided, at the bottom of the balcony stairway for a full minute before making his way into the sanctuary to sit with his family. A decision he'd been regretting ever since, even as he had to acknowledge to himself that this was probably how Ava preferred it.

Simeon elbowed him as the congregation sat. Joseph followed a beat later, forcing his attention to the pulpit, where Pastor Cooper, the youth pastor who served with Dad, was getting ready to preach. The guy was his sister Grace's age—Mama had even wanted Grace to marry him at one point—and an engaging preacher, though in a different way from Dad.

"I am about the most impatient person you ever met," Pastor Cooper opened his sermon. "I cannot handle waiting in a line. Can't handle waiting for deliveries. Honestly, I can't even handle waiting for someone to reply to my texts."

*Amen to that.* Joseph smiled ironically. Waiting for a text could just about kill a man. Which was part of the reason he hadn't texted Ava after Friday night. His heart wasn't prepared to wait right now.

"And waiting on an answer to a prayer. Ooh boy." Pastor Cooper wiped his brow in exaggeration. "I really can't handle that." He stepped down from the pulpit and walked closer to the congregation. "How about y'all? You ever feel like God is slow as a snail in molasses to answer your prayers?"

Make that a snail crawling *backwards* through molasses, and Pastor Cooper might be onto something.

"But you know," Pastor Cooper continued. "I don't think any of us really have a right to complain. Not unless you've prayed for something as long as Abraham and Sarah did. They waited a looong time for God to keep his promise to bless them with a child–until they were in their nineties. Or what about Hannah? She waited a long time for her answered prayer. Zechariah and Elizabeth too. Talk about patience. It makes me itchy to think about all the waiting." He shook his head. "You ever wonder if they felt that way sometimes–itchy with waiting? Discouraged with impatience? I dunno." He shrugged, lifting his hands to his sides. "Probably. I mean, they were human like you and me. But here's what they did in their impatience–" Pastor Cooper paused long enough that Joseph started to feel impatient for him to continue.

But then the young pastor smiled. "They waited on the Lord. They trusted in his timing."

Joseph sank back into the pew. It felt like he'd been waiting forever already for God to answer his prayers about Ava. But what if this wasn't God's timing? What if it was never God's timing for them to be together?

"I can hear the question half of y'all are thinking right now," Pastor Cooper said. "The other half of you are wondering how long you'll have to wait for me to wrap this sermon up." A laugh went through the church. "But the half of y'all who aren't feeling so impatient with me, you're wondering how you know the difference between God's 'wait' and his 'no.' Should you wait a certain number of days or weeks or years and then figure it must be a no?"

Pastor Cooper looked thoughtfully at the congregation. "I don't think so. Remember, God doesn't work on our timelines. To him, a thousand years are like a day. Abraham's one hundred years was no time at all to God."

Joseph shook his head to himself. In another hundred years, he and Ava would be beyond the nursing home.

But Pastor Cooper was still preaching. "So we wait on the Lord, boldly, confidently, trusting in him fully. And as we wait, we worship, we serve, we glorify. And when he answers those prayers, whether with a yes, a no, or a wait some more, we give him thanks that though we are impatient, he is patient. He coulda—probably shoulda—wiped us all out from the start, from that first sin. But he waited. He promised a Savior. He waited some more. He sent that Savior. He waited some more. He promises to bring all who believe in him to eternal glory in heaven. So why all the waiting? Why not just snap his fingers and take care of it all in one moment—I mean, he's God, nothing is too hard for him, right? But here's the reason for his patience: You. Me."

Pastor Cooper strode back to the pulpit and looked down at the Bible Joseph knew always rested there. "The Lord is not slow in keeping his promises, as some understand slowness. Instead he is patient with you, not wanting anyone to perish, but everyone to come to repentance." He looked up. "It's the ultimate patience. Waiting for us to turn and repent. To believe that he has taken away our sins. So that one day all of our impatience will disappear as we are in the never-ending joy of eternity with him. Amen."

This time as he stood, Joseph couldn't help looking over his shoulder at the balcony.

Lori was wiping her eyes and smiling, and next to her, Ava looked radiant. Joseph's heart filled with joy for her. She'd been waiting so long for Lori to be willing to come to church with her, to listen to God's Word. He could only imagine how strongly Pastor Cooper's sermon must have resonated with her.

He turned back toward the altar, his heart suddenly lighter.

He could wait on the Lord.

And on Ava.

"Come on, we have to go," Ava whispered, tugging urgently on Aunt Lori's hand as Pastor Cooper began his weekly announcements at the end of the service.

"What? Why?" Lori whispered, tugging back and remaining in her seat.

Well, that was cute. Ava had been waiting sixteen years for her aunt to come to church and now that she had, she didn't want to leave.

"I can't." Ava directed her eyes pointedly to the pews below—to Joseph, who was right there and yet so far out of reach.

"Ava, I think you should at least—"

But Ava tugged harder, and Lori practically fell out of her seat. She gave Ava a look but stood and followed as she tiptoed down the steps at full speed, then launched herself out the church doors and made a beeline for Lori's car.

"Lori." The voice called her aunt's name when they were halfway across the parking lot. "Can we talk a minute?"

Aunt Lori glanced at Ava, a question in her eyes. Ava bit her lip, looking over her shoulder at the church doors. Mr. Germain was the only one out there, but others would follow soon.

She desperately wanted to say that now was not the time. Lori could talk to Mr. Germain later. Somewhere else.

But she nodded. "I'll be in the car."

Lori squeezed her hand with a grateful smile. "I won't be long."

Ava practically ran the rest of the way to the car, then slouched down as far as she could in her seat, eyes fixed all the while on the church building, as she prayed that Joseph wouldn't come out.

She owed him an apology for Friday night. But she couldn't face him right now. Wasn't sure how she'd face him ever again.

Her eyes strayed to Lori and Mr. Germain, who had rested a hand on her aunt's arm. He appeared to be speaking earnestly, and as Ava watched, Lori smiled, then leaned over to hug him.

Ava wrapped her arms around her middle as the ache in her heart deepened. Why was it so easy for everyone else and so hard for her?

When Aunt Lori returned to the car, she was beaming.

"So?" Ava let herself sit up enough to fasten her seat belt.

"He said he wants me to be part of his decision. We're going to have dinner tonight to talk about things."

"That's great." Ava sat up all the way as Lori finally pulled out of the parking lot, though she waited until they were two blocks down the street to breathe again.

As she did, an unwanted wave of disappointment rolled over her.

Joseph hadn't followed her out the way Mr. Germain had followed Aunt Lori. He hadn't come looking for her at all.

*How many times can you push him away and expect him to come back?*

She knew that was true. And she hadn't wanted him to come after her. So she needed to stop moping.

"So," she said to Lori, "how did you like the service?" She felt strangely shy, asking the question, like the first time she'd shown Lori one of her photographs.

Instead of the enthusiastic yes Lori had given the picture, she nodded slowly. "I . . . It was . . ." She swallowed. "It was good. I guess I never really thought of God like that—patient. Waiting for us. Loving us. Forgiving us." She shook her head. "I'm not saying I'll go all the time. But I think I'd like to hear more."

If Ava hadn't been buckled in, she would have jumped up and danced. Or crushed Lori in a hug. Pastor Cooper had certainly been right about that whole waiting on the Lord thing.

She remembered what Joseph had said. He had been praying that she would change her mind about dating him. When she'd finally said yes, he must have felt the same way she did right now.

Until she'd ruined it.

No doubt he'd have no patience for her now.

# Chapter 34

Joseph was lying on the couch Tuesday night, unable to work up the energy to order a pizza, when his doorbell rang. A firework of hope launched in his chest as he sprang to his feet.

*Ava?*

He'd texted her earlier to ask if they could talk, but she'd never responded. Because she'd wanted to talk in person?

As he charged toward the door, his eyes caught on the dishes scattered uncharacteristically across the living room. He should probably clean up first, but he didn't have time for that right now. He had to see her.

He ran a quick hand over his hair as he pulled the door open but dropped it as his eyes met the woman standing there. "Oh."

Lori laughed. "Sorry to disappoint."

"Yeah." Joseph ran a hand over his hair again. He'd gotten the distinct impression ever since he'd returned to River Falls that Ava's aunt no longer approved of him as she had when he and Ava were in high school. He wondered briefly if she was in part to blame for Ava's hesitation to be with him. "Sorry. I thought maybe you were—"

"Ava. Yeah. I know. I saw your text."

"You did?" And had Ava seen it? But he didn't ask.

"Could I come in for a minute?"

"Um. I guess?" He had a very bad feeling about this, but he stepped aside and gestured toward the living room, stacking bowls and plates as he followed her. "Sorry about the mess."

But Lori didn't answer as she took a seat on the edge of the couch. Joseph remained on his feet, watching her.

After a moment, he remembered the manners his mama had drilled into him. "Can I get you something to drink?"

"What? Oh. No thank you." Lori rubbed a finger back and forth across her lip—he wondered if she got that from Ava or Ava got that from her.

"Look, Joseph," she said abruptly, and his defenses instantly came up. She was going to tell him to leave Ava alone.

"I know this is long overdue," Lori continued. "But I owe you an apology."

Joseph gaped at her. She was *apologizing* to him? "For what?"

He didn't realize he'd asked the question out loud until she said, "I never thanked you for saving Ava. That night."

"You don't have to—"

Lori held up a hand. "Yes I do. I was angry with you for the way you left Ava afterward—"

"She—"

Her hand came up again. "I know now that she was the one who broke up with you. But even when I didn't know, I should have thanked you. She's the most important person in the world to me—"

"To me too." This time he wasn't going to let her stop him. "I would do anything for her."

Lori studied him for a moment, as if trying to assess the truth of his statement. Finally, she said, "I know you would."

"If she'd let me." He couldn't help the semi-bitter laugh. How hard was it to let someone love you?

"I know. She's a stubborn one, our Ava."

Joseph grinned at that. He liked the sound of it, "our Ava."

"Is there anything I can do?" he asked, not caring if his desperation was obvious.

Lori worried her lip, then looked up at him with a gleam in her eyes. "Can you cook?"

Joseph nodded, then stopped. "Sort of. I have a great chicken cacciatore recipe. But it's not like she's going to agree to come to dinner. She practically ran away from me the other night."

"Leave that to me." Lori sprang to her feet, dusting off her hands as if she were going to get to work. "You just make the chicken." She glanced around, wrinkling her nose. "And maybe clean up a bit."

Joseph's laugh felt light and full of hope. He was going to do better than clean up a bit. He was going to make it magical.

# Chapter 35

"Well, girls, I think we might pull this off." The dogs watched intently as Joseph stirred the chicken, then gave everything a final once-over.

Patio table set for two. Check. Candles and hanging lights. Check. Soft music. Check. Suit and tie. Check. Shoes.

*Shoes.*

That was what he was missing.

Laughing at himself, he opened the back door to let the dogs out, then hurried to the closet to get his dress shoes.

He still wasn't quite sure how Lori was going to convince Ava to come. But he had no choice but to trust that she would.

He paused with one shoe on, offering a prayer that God would bless their night together. That he would give Joseph wisdom to show love and patience for Ava. That—

A wild yowling from outside interrupted his prayer and drove him to the door with one shoe on and one shoe off.

The smell hit him first.

Pungent. Acrid. Rotten.

He covered his mouth with his hand, his eyes watering at the strength of it.

Skunk.

He stepped outside to find the dogs slinking toward the house.

"Yeah. You better look ashamed," he called to them. "How am I supposed to explain this to Ava?"

"Come on. Let's go."

Ava looked up from the book she'd been reading, squinting at Lori. Sometime between when Ava had started reading and now, dusk had fallen, but Ava had been so absorbed in the book that she hadn't thought to turn the lights on.

"Go where?" She closed the book over her finger. She'd showered and changed into her pajamas right after she'd come home from the studio. Preparation for a big Friday night at home.

"That's for me to know and you to find out." Lori smirked at her. "Come on."

Ava crossed her arms. She wasn't bothering to get up and get dressed for anything less than a—

Nope. There was nothing she would be willing to get up and get dressed for right now.

"Fine." Lori rolled her eyes. "It was supposed to be a surprise, but Michael has a friend who has a dog he can't keep anymore, and I said we'd—"

Ava sprang off the couch. "Seriously? We're getting another dog?" She thought guiltily of Princess. If she was going to bring another dog home, it should be the pup she'd come to think of as her own already. But that would mean having to see Joseph. Anyway, Princess was plenty happy with him. This way, she could have a dog that was wholly hers, no strings attached.

She followed Lori to the car, asking a million questions about what kind of dog it was, how old it was, what had made Lori change her mind about getting another dog.

But Lori refused to say another word—though her smile grew bigger the closer they got to River Falls. It wasn't until she gave up asking questions and turned to look out the window that Ava caught a glimpse of her reflection and realized she'd already washed off her makeup. She patted her face, feeling suddenly naked and vulnerable.

But it wasn't like she was going to compete in a beauty contest. She was going to get a dog—who wouldn't care one bit what her face looked like. She forced herself to let her breath out and think about something else.

"I take it your dinner with Mr. Germain went well the other night then?"

Ava's and Lori's schedules had seemed to conflict all week, and Ava had barely seen her aunt since Sunday.

"It did." Lori's voice was full with her smile. "He asked if I'd be willing to stay together, either way."

"What does that mean?" Ava frowned. "Like you would move to Nebraska?"

Lori shrugged. "Maybe. Eventually. Not right away. Not unless we were . . ." For the first time in Ava's life, Lori looked shy. "Married."

"Wow." Ava tried to take that in. For so long, Aunt Lori had been the only person in her life. And now she might get married and leave.

"I mean, it wouldn't be for a long time yet," Lori rushed to add. "We'd probably do a long-distance thing first. And that's if he even takes the job . . ." Lori trailed off, but Ava's attention had been snagged by the street they'd just turned onto.

A pit opened in her stomach. "Mr. Germain's friend lives on the same street as Joseph?"

"Well . . ." Lori slowed the car.

And Ava knew. "Take me home, Lori." Her voice cracked, and she clutched the door handle. "Right now."

Lori shook her head. "You have to stop pushing him away, Ava. He loves you. And you love him. Even if your thick skull won't let you admit it."

Ava grasped at her cheek. "I don't have makeup on."

"He doesn't care about that, Ava," Lori said gently. "And I think you know that."

"I—" She clapped a hand over her mouth and nose as a strong odor invaded the car. "What is that?" she asked around her fingers.

"Skunk, I think." Lori slowed and turned into Joseph's driveway. "And it's stronger here." She put the car in park, then passed Ava a paper shopping bag. "You're going to need this."

Ava lowered her hand from her face so she could open it, but Lori stopped her. "Wait until it's time."

"Time?" Seriously, this night couldn't get any weirder.

"Just go." Lori shooed Ava out of the car. "And remember, stop pushing him away."

Ava swallowed. What would Lori do if she refused to go inside? Come around and pull her out of the car by force?

Ava would like to see her try.

But as Ava studied the house, looked at the little flower bed out front where Princess liked to dig, focused on the porch steps where she and Joseph had talked, she realized that she *did* want to go in there. To apologize to him for running out of the restaurant last weekend, if nothing else. Or maybe to—

*No. Nothing else.*

With a sigh, she pushed the car door open, the stench of skunk immediately intensifying. Trying to avoid inhaling, she made her way to the porch, clutching the mystery bag in her hands, as Aunt Lori drove away.

With a deep breath that she immediately regretted as the smell of skunk musk coated her tongue, she pressed the doorbell. There was an instant racket inside—barking, a scramble of claws on hardwood, a yell, and more barking.

The moment Joseph opened the door, Ava burst into laughter. Who said the night couldn't get any weirder?

Both dogs were dripping wet, their fur sticking up in odd spikes. Joseph was soaked too, his white dress shirt half tucked and half untucked—and his hair stood up in adorable spikes. But the funniest part was the look on his face—pure consternation.

"What have y'all been doing?" Ava asked as both Tasha and Princess rubbed their wet bodies against her legs.

"I am so sorry." Joseph gestured for her to come inside. "Everything was all ready and perfect, but these two decided they needed to make friends with a skunk. It didn't want to make friends back."

Simultaneously, the dogs shook off, sending water droplets flying across the room—and onto both Ava and Joseph.

"I was able to get the smell mostly out of them with a baking soda and peroxide mixture, but it smells so terrible outside that I don't think we can eat out there like I was planning." He pointed toward the doors that led to the patio outside, where Ava could see a table still set for two—complete with candles and romantic lights. "Not that there's any food," Joseph continued. "I was so busy with the dogs, I burnt the chicken cacciatore to a crisp, so . . ."

"It's okay." She reached out a hand to him without thinking, letting her fingers rest on his wet sleeve. "This is really . . ." She looked around again. "You went to a lot of trouble for me."

Joseph held her gaze. "I would do anything for you. And if that means never going out again, if it means cooking for you and cleaning up for you and even washing the skunk out of dogs for you, I'll do it. Whatever it means, I'll do it."

That was . . . wow.

Ava had to take a step backwards to breathe, though she wasn't sure if that was from the intensity of his words or the intensity of his scent. "Why don't you go get changed? You're soaked. And you smell a little skunky, no offense."

Joseph laughed and pointed at the bag she still clutched in her hand. "And you should probably look in there." He disappeared down the hallway, calling over his shoulder, "I'll change in my room. You can use the bathroom."

Ava peered after him, puzzled. She didn't need to use the bathroom. She turned her attention to the bag, opening it and reaching inside, a gasp slipping from her as she pulled out a shimmery, silver dress—the one she'd been planning to wear to prom with Joseph. Ava hadn't even realized she still had it. She'd figured Lori had tossed it out long ago.

She ran her fingers over the silky fabric, letting herself wonder if it would still fit.

"Ava?" Joseph called from down the hallway.

"Coming." She made her way toward his voice and found him standing in the door to his bedroom, his dress shirt unbuttoned and untucked around the t-shirt he wore beneath it.

"You don't have to wear the dress if you don't want to," he said. "You look perfect just the way you are."

Ava glanced down at her clothes, suddenly realizing that she was wearing her pajamas and no makeup. But instead of embarrassment or horror or fear, all she felt was relief. Joseph had seen her the way she really was—and he hadn't run away screaming.

"I just thought it might be fun to . . ." Joseph's brow wrinkled, as if he was afraid he'd offended her. "But considering that we're probably going to end up ordering pizza, maybe it's kind of silly."

Ava skimmed her fingers over the dress again. "I want to wear it."

Joseph could not stop staring at Ava. Not only because she looked breath-stoppingly beautiful in the flowing silver dress that set off her green eyes and delicate shoulders but also because he couldn't believe she was really here. Couldn't believe she was eating pizza and smiling at him over the candles he'd rescued from the patio. Couldn't believe she hadn't gone running the moment she'd arrived at his house and smelled the skunk.

As they finished their dinner, he reached for her plate, accidentally brushing her hand. She didn't flinch but smiled.

It gave him courage. "I was thinking." He stood and carried their plates to the sink. He may have been feeling brave, but not quite brave enough to look at her as he asked. "We never got to dance. At prom, I mean."

"That's true." Ava's voice didn't hold its usually guarded quality, which gave him just enough confidence to ask the rest.

"So I thought maybe we could now?"

Ava didn't answer right away, and his confidence dipped. "Or we don't have to. We could play chess or watch a movie or—"

"Joseph—" Ava interrupted. "I'd like to dance with you. It's just . . ."

He looked up to find her tugging at a strand of hair.

"I've never danced with a boy," she said shyly.

Joseph's laugh boomed loud enough to make Princess spring excitedly to her feet and prance toward him. "Sure you have. Remember in middle school? You danced with Stewart Block. I was so jealous."

Now Ava was laughing too. "You're right, I did. I couldn't walk for a week afterward, he stomped my feet so many times."

"Well, I promise not to stomp." He stepped toward her and held out a hand, holding his breath as she eyed it.

Finally, her hand landed in his, and a zap of familiarity mingled with anticipation flowed up his arm. With his other hand, he opened the song he already had queued on his phone.

As the first strains of music floated toward them, he set the phone on the table and gathered her to him. Her jasmine scent surrounded him as her hands came to his shoulders, and all he could do for a moment was breathe in and hold her tight.

As the first verse of the song started, he forced himself to move his feet.

"Is this . . ." Ava pulled back a little.

"Our song." He'd been driving her home from Bible study one night when the song had come on the radio.

"This is our song," she'd said, turning up the volume. Not really understanding the point of having an "our song," but wanting her to be happy, Joseph had agreed. Over the past eight years, he'd been glad of it—every time he heard the song, it reminded him that love could outlast anything.

"Joseph." Ava's whisper was strangled.

He stopped swaying but didn't let go of her. "What is it, Ava?"

"We can't go back." She looked away from him. "We can't be who we used to be."

Joseph tightened his hold on her. "I know."

She turned her eyes on him. "You know?"

He nodded. "I've been thinking a lot about what you said the other night. About how you're not the same Ava you were then. And I realized, you're right."

"Oh." Ava's face fell, and she tried to pull away from him, but he held her tight.

"You're not the same Ava. And I'm not the same Joseph either. We're both older. Both wiser, hopefully. Both carrying new hurts and scars."

She nodded, and her lip trembled.

"But—" He moved his hand to her cheek. "None of that changes my feelings for you. If anything, it makes me want to spend more time with you. Get to know new Ava even better."

Ava brought her gaze to his. "And what if you don't like new Ava?" she whispered.

"Oh, trust me—" He let his thumb caress her cheek. "I like new Ava a whole lot. In fact—" he tilted his head closer to hers. "I love her."

Ava inhaled sharply. “Joseph, don’t say—”

“I love you, Ava.” He let his lips touch hers, gently, testing. When hers responded, he pulled her closer, letting himself get lost in every sensation.

One thing this kiss made him sure of: Ava might be a different person. And he might be too. But they had never been more right for each other.

# Chapter 36

"You're sure you're comfortable with this?"

Ava laughed as Joseph parked the car in the parking lot of Beautiful Savior and turned toward her, his brow creased with worry. It was the tenth time he'd asked in the last hour. Which was sweet—but not necessary.

"It's your brother's wedding, Joseph. Of course I'm comfortable with it." She pulled on the sweater she planned to wear over her dress—not so much to hide her scars but because early December in River Falls could be chilly. "Now let's get inside so they don't think their photographer has bailed on them." In general, Ava avoided doing wedding photos—there were far too many people at a wedding—but she'd made an exception when Asher and Ireland had asked.

Joseph caught her hand before she could open her car door. She turned a scolding look on him. "Seriously, Joseph, we have to—"

"I know. I just wanted to say thank you."

Ava raised an eyebrow. "I haven't taken the pictures yet," she joked.

But Joseph looked uncharacteristically serious. "I mean thank you for giving us another chance. The past few months have been . . ." Joseph gazed out the window toward the church, then back at her. "The best of my life. Ever."

"Me too." Ava could only whisper as the full impact of his words hit her.

He leaned forward and brought his lips to hers. "I love you," he said as they pulled apart.

Ava swallowed. He'd said it so many times. And she wanted to get the words out—so badly. Because she did love him. That had never been in question. The question was, what would happen if she said it out loud?

She pushed her door open. "Come on. It looks like the bride and groom are here."

"Hey, bro, you know this is supposed to be a party, right?" Asher stopped in front of Joseph's otherwise empty table, his arm wrapped firmly around his bride's waist.

Joseph stood, giving first Ireland then his brother a quick hug. "Congratulations. It was a beautiful day."

"So why aren't you dancing?" Ireland swayed to the music.

"My date's a little busy." Joseph nodded toward Ava, who had her camera lifted to her face—same as she had all day.

"Oh. Uh uh." Ireland slipped out of Asher's arms, pausing to kiss him. "Be right back." Then she strode straight for Ava.

Asher nudged Joseph. "Bet she gets Ava over here in thirty seconds flat."

Joseph laughed half-heartedly. He wasn't sure if it mattered. Not if Ava was going to keep sidestepping his declarations of love. Not if she kept holding him at arm's length.

It wasn't that she'd shut him out. They spent time together nearly every day, called each other when they were apart, kissed whenever they had a moment. And it was all wonderful. But it all left him yearning for more.

More of her heart.

More of her trust.

More of *her*.

But it was a *more* he was starting to wonder if she could give.

"Hey, man. Everything's okay between you two, right?" Asher asked.

Joseph nodded. "Yeah, of course. I just wish it was a little easier, you know? Like it is for you and Ireland."

Asher snorted. "Tell me you're kidding." He elbowed Joseph as Ireland led Ava toward them. "I don't think any relationship is necessarily easy. It takes work. But it's totally worth it."

"Well, coming from someone who vowed not three years ago to be a perennial bachelor, I guess that means a lot." Joseph shoved his brother's arm.

Asher grinned as Ireland pulled Ava up to them.

"One wedding date. As promised." Ireland nudged Ava toward him before taking Asher's hand. "Come on. We still have that whole side of the room to say hi to."

"Wait," Ava cried, and Joseph winced. Was she that desperate not to be alone with him?

She pulled her camera strap from around her neck and held the device out to Asher. "Would you take a picture of us?"

Joseph gaped at her. She wanted to have her picture taken?

"You're sure?" He turned his back on the camera, shielding her from it. He didn't want her to do this if she wasn't comfortable with it.

"I'm sure. We're going to want to remember this night, right?" She took his hand and positioned him on her left, then angled herself into him, so that her scarred side faced away from the camera.

The shutter clicked a few times before Asher lowered it. He stepped toward them, holding the camera out to Ava, but before she could take it, Joseph pulled her into a kiss.

Somewhere far in the background, he could hear Asher clearing his throat and Ireland giggling and music playing and people talking. But he was focused on only one thing: this incredible, brave, wonderful woman in front of him.

When he finally let her go, Asher bumped his arm with the camera. "Now that's the kind of work I'm talking about."

Ava gave him a puzzled look, and Joseph shook his head. "Never mind him."

As Asher and Ireland melted into the crowd of guests, Ava fiddled with the dials on her camera, and Joseph's heart, floating only a second ago, crashed to earth. Was she going to go back to hiding behind her camera now?

"I'll be right back, okay?" She squeezed his arm. "You'll be right here?"

He nodded, waiting until she'd disappeared among the bodies to sit with a sigh. He leaned back in his seat. He might as well get comfortable. Who knew how long she'd be off taking pictures this time.

"Hey, man." Zeb pulled out the chair next to him. "Where's Ava off to? She looked like she was in a hurry."

Joseph shrugged. Away from him, that was all he knew.

"Look, I just wanted to say that I know I gave you a hard time about being with her again and feelings changing and all that. But I'm glad you ignored me. I was obviously wrong."

Joseph shrugged again. What if he was the one who'd been wrong?

"Hello? Is this thing on?" Zeb pretended to tap an invisible microphone in front of him. "I'm saying I was wrong, and you were right. Doesn't happen often."

Joseph made himself laugh. "Thanks, Zeb. I appreciate it. But—"

"Hey, Zeb." Ava rushed to the table, camera nowhere in sight. "Mind if I steal Joseph away?"

"He's all yours." Zeb slapped Joseph's shoulder as he stood. Then he turned to Ava and gave her a quick hug. She looked surprised, but hugged him back.

As soon as Zeb had walked away, Ava held out a hand to Joseph. "Take a walk with me?" That smile—it was warm and tantalizing and . . . something else he couldn't put his finger on—something he wanted to know more about.

"Okay?" Joseph took her hand and stood. "Where's your camera?"

"I locked it up. Ireland made it clear that I was under no circumstances to take any more pictures tonight."

Joseph frowned. "She doesn't want pictures of the reception?"

"I got all the important ones already. Anyway, I think it was more that she didn't want her new brother-in-law to be neglected any longer. Sorry we had to spend so much of the day apart."

Joseph shrugged as if he hadn't just been moping about that very thing. "So, where are you taking me?"

"You'll see." There was that smile again. She was clearly enjoying being mysterious.

She led him to a set of glass doors, beyond which there was a large, lighted patio. He opened the door for her and followed her outside.

The temperature had fallen with the sun, and Joseph drew in a breath of the crisp December air. It fogged in front of his face as he blew it back out. This had always been his favorite time of the year, and he was incredibly grateful suddenly to be standing here with his favorite person.

Ava took his hand and led him past the small clusters of guests on the patio toward a cobblestone path that led in a winding route through spruce trees wrapped with white lights, down to the river's edge. They made their way toward another, smaller, more intimate patio, covered by a pergola strung with more lights.

Neither of them said anything as they walked, and Joseph let himself stop worrying for once about what was going to come next and just savor the moment.

When they reached the patio, he wrapped an arm around Ava's shoulders and snugged her close. "You're cold." He let go and started to take off his suit coat, but she grabbed his hand.

"I'm not cold, Joseph. I'm . . ." She licked her lips, that smile never faltering. "I'm in love with you. And I don't know why it's taken me so long to tell you. I guess I just—"

Ava's words got lost as Joseph's lips met hers, though she honestly couldn't say whether she had moved to kiss him or he had moved to kiss her or they had moved to kiss each other. What she could say was that she had been a fool to wait to tell him. Because now that she'd said it once, she wanted to say it again and again and again.

She pulled away for a moment, and Joseph gave her a questioning look.

"I just wanted to say it again." She grinned at him. "I love you."

Joseph's grin faded, and he looked suddenly grave.

Ava's heart faltered. Why wasn't he saying it back? Why wasn't he saying anything? "Joseph?"

He dropped his hands from her shoulders and led her to a stone bench at the edge of the patio, gesturing for her to sit. She obeyed, a strange flutter going through her tummy, though she couldn't say why. He took off his coat and wrapped it over her shoulders, then lowered himself onto the bench next to her, taking both of her hands in his. "Do you remember the promise we made each other?" His tone was urgent, as if he was afraid she'd forgotten.

She swallowed and nodded.

Of course she remembered. But they'd only been eighteen. It didn't mean . . .

"I want to keep that promise, Ava. I want to spend forever with you."

Ava sucked in a sharp breath. Forever was a big word. A word she'd thought had been shattered into pieces the night of the fire.

In one fluid motion, Joseph slipped off the bench and dropped to one knee right there on the patio.

"Joseph—" She choked on his name. What was he doing? He couldn't do this.

He gave her a sheepish grin. "I'm sorry. I don't have a ring. I mean, I do. Have a ring. But it's at home. I was planning to wait." He laughed self-consciously. "I was trying to be patient. But I have to ask this right now. Ava, will you marry me?" The steam from his breath hung in the air, seeming to hold the words in front of her.

"Henry, come back here—" A woman's voice pulled Ava's gaze to the lawn just in time to see a little boy barreling down the path toward them.

"I want to see the boats," the boy called, still running at full tilt as his feet hit the patio. He stopped abruptly as he spotted them. "Whatcha doin'?" he asked Joseph. "Did you lose something? I dropped my tooth once, and we didn't find it until Mama stepped on it."

Joseph laughed as a woman swooped in and held out a hand to the child. "Henry, come here." She smiled at Joseph. "I am so sorry to interrupt." Her eyes went to Ava, then darted quickly away, but not before Ava spotted the look of pity. "Congratulations."

"But Mama, I wanna see the boats," the little boy wailed as the woman scooped him up and passed him to a man who had come down the hill behind them.

The woman gestured toward her and Joseph, and Ava saw the man's face turn their way. She swiveled her head so he wouldn't spot her scars too.

"Ava?" Joseph's voice beckoned to her, but she couldn't look away from the boy and his parents. They made a striking image under the twinkle lights: mom, dad, and child—all of them perfect.

Ava's eyes roved up the hill to the reception hall. It was filled with people just like them. Perfect people. People who belonged.

That was what Joseph deserved. He didn't deserve a wife who would cause people to give him pitying looks. And his children certainly didn't deserve a mother they wouldn't want to be seen in public with. One they'd have to make explanations and excuses for.

"Ava?" Joseph's finger came to her chin, turning her toward him. "What is it?"

She bit her lip, looking from him to the family walking away from the river. She wanted to say yes. So badly that she could feel the ache of it clear through her body. But that wouldn't be fair to Joseph.

He deserved a normal life with a normal woman.

"I don't—" She whispered, then broke off. Her lips quivered, and she closed her eyes, but the tears still seeped out. She couldn't look at him as she said it. "I don't know."

Joseph didn't let go of her hands. Didn't get up and walk away. Didn't say anything.

After a moment, she couldn't stand it anymore. She had to open her eyes.

He was watching her, and nothing in his expression had changed. That love was still there.

"That's okay," he said simply. "But just so you know, I'm not going anywhere this time. No matter how long it takes. Because one thing I know—you're worth waiting for."

# Chapter 37

"How was the wedding last night?" Aunt Lori bustled into the kitchen, grinning from ear to ear.

"I– It was–" A sob ripped out of Ava's chest, and she pressed a hand to her mouth to keep any more from escaping.

Aunt Lori's grin changed to alarm, and Ava could only gulp in a breath as Lori rushed to her side and wrapped her arms around her.

When she could finally talk, she said, "He asked me–" She hiccupped around another almost-sob. "To marry him."

"I can see why that's so upsetting." The sarcasm in Lori's voice stung Ava.

She shook her head. "I don't expect you to understand."

Lori stepped back, standing in front of Ava, until Ava had no choice but to look at her. "What?"

Lori's arms were crossed, her face set. "Do you really think you're the only one who has imperfections? The only one who feels like life hasn't been fair?"

"I don't feel like–"

But Lori's look silenced her. "You blame Joseph for being caught up in the past. But it's you, Ava. You're the one who thinks if you can't be that perfect girl you used to be, no one will want you. But I have news for you: you weren't perfect then and you aren't perfect now. And neither is Joseph. And neither am I and neither is Michael. Or anyone. And yet we love each other anyway. That's a gift. From God, I imagine. So before you go throwing it away, maybe you should think about that. I'm going to go get ready for church." Lori strode away, leaving Ava feeling both as if she'd just received the scolding of her life and as if she'd completely deserved it.

"Oh, and by the way—" Lori stopped in the kitchen doorway. "Michael asked me to marry him last night. Or well, technically, I asked him. Or well— The point is, we both said yes."

"What?" Ava was certain she'd heard wrong.

But the grin that burst onto Lori's face confirmed the words.

Ava sprang from her chair and threw herself across the room to hug her aunt. "I'm so happy for you. But what— How—" She blew out a breath. "You know what, tell me on the way to church. I need to go get dressed."

Joseph set the dogs on a grueling pace toward his and Ava's park. His legs pumped hard, though exhaustion pulled at his limbs after being up until the wee hours to help transport Asher and Ireland's wedding gifts. And then he'd spent the rest of the night in and out of sleep, praying every time he woke up that God would give him peace with whatever Ava decided. That he would give them both clarity.

He reached the park in record time and pulled the dogs to a halt. He unclipped their leashes to let them explore, then lifted his hands to his head, elbows out, waiting for his breathing to slow.

Wisps of vapor hovered above the glassy surface of the river, its current barely discernible in the soft morning light that reflected the leafless tree limbs.

He tilted his head back, taking in the flawless blue of the sky, the trill of the birds waking, the smell of the cold, fresh air. A finger of light burst through the bare trees across the river, landing on his face.

And a powerful realization came over him: this was God's creation. Every last bird, every last tree, every last wisp of fog.

"All right, Lord," he prayed. "I get it. You are all powerful. You made all of this. You made us. You know what is best for us. Help me to trust you in this. To wait peacefully. And to submit to your will, whether she says yes or no. To love her as you love me, no matter what. In Jesus' name, Amen."

He stood there, just watching the river, until the dogs bounded back to his side.

"All right, girls. Let's go home." Peace settled over him as he started toward home at a slower pace.

God showed him patience every day.

And he would do the same for Ava, no matter how long it took.

When he got home, he took a quick shower, then dressed for church and ate a piece of toast, throwing the crusts to the dogs.

"I'll be back to pick you up after church," he reassured Tasha as he put his dress shoes on. They were going to the Children's Hospital today for an early Christmas party. He glanced at the piles of presents he and Ava had shopped for together over the past few weeks and then spent evenings wrapping together. The whole time, he'd felt like it was a rehearsal for someday, when they had kids of their own to shop and wrap for. The whole time, the ring had sat in his dresser, just waiting for him to pull it out and ask her. But he'd known she wasn't ready yet.

Maybe she never would be.

But just in case . . .

He jogged back to the bedroom and grabbed the little velvet bag with the ring out of the drawer, tucking it into his pocket. He'd keep it with him until she made a decision. But he wouldn't pressure her.

Patting it one last time, he said goodbye to the dogs and jumped into his car.

# Chapter 38

"I'm so happy for you," Ava said again as Lori finished telling about how she'd spontaneously burst out in the middle of dinner last night that she thought they should get married. And how Mr. Germain hadn't hesitated even a second before saying yes, of course they should and then going on to ask her to marry him. And how they'd then argued about who had proposed to whom.

"There's one other thing," Lori said hesitantly.

"I know." Ava had been going to the school to help Mr. Germain—she supposed she'd better get used to calling him Michael now—with the yearbook club for a couple months now, and he'd told her weeks ago that he'd decided to take the job in Nebraska. The truth was, she'd been expecting something like this ever since.

"We talked about it, and we both agreed that if you want to come to Nebraska with us, there's a place for you. Of course, I understand that there might be certain, uh, things that make you want to stay here, but you could start a studio there or . . ." Lori cast her a worried glance.

Ava reached over to squeeze her aunt's arm. "That is so sweet of you. Of both of you. But my place is here. And you've put your life on hold for me long enough. It's time for you to get out and live a little."

Lori let out a breath. "And what are you going to do? About Joseph?"

Ava shook her head. She'd spent her entire shower this morning praying for clarity. But somehow, she only felt more confused than ever. She knew she loved him. Knew he loved her. She knew he wanted her to say yes. Knew she wanted to say yes. And yet, she couldn't get over the nagging feeling that it would be selfish. That he deserved more.

"Speaking of . . ." Aunt Lori nodded toward the church doors as she pulled into Beautiful Savior's parking lot. "Looks like someone couldn't wait to see you."

A ripple of nerves went through Ava as she spotted Joseph waiting in front of the building. As soon as his head turned their direction, he broke into a smile and sprinted their way.

A brief flash of panic went through her. He wasn't going to expect her to have an answer right this minute, was he?

The moment Lori put the car in park, Joseph was pulling Ava's door open.

She got out slowly, suddenly shy, not knowing how he was going to feel about her after last night.

"Good morning," she said softly.

"Good morning." He stepped forward, lowering his face toward hers but stopping to give her a questioning look. Was this okay with her?

She nodded and smiled and lifted her face to his.

"All right, you two. There will be time for that later." Lori walked up next to them. "Come on. Let's get inside before the service starts."

Ava smiled as she and Joseph pulled apart, and she slipped her hand into his. "Aunt Lori and Mr. Germain are getting married."

"What?" Joseph stopped and held out a hand to Lori. "Congratulations."

Lori looked at his hand, then ignored it and wrapped him in a hug.

Well.

Would wonders never cease?

Ava could count on three fingers the number of people she'd ever seen Aunt Lori hug. She pressed her hands together under her chin, her heart nearly bursting.

Lori whispered something to Joseph that Ava couldn't make out.

He pulled back and grinned at her. "Never."

"Never what?" Ava asked.

Still grinning, Joseph took her hand. "Never you mind."

Before Ava could press the question, the bell chimed.

Lori waved to them. "I'm going to go sit with my fiancé if you two don't mind."

"Tell him I said congratulations," Ava called after her, and Joseph added, "Me too."

They hurried inside, and Joseph turned toward the steps to the balcony, where they always sat.

But Ava tugged him back. "Let's sit with your family."

"Yeah?" He scrutinized her. "You think that will be okay?"

She squeezed his hand. "I'll be fine as long as you're with me."

"I'll always be with you." He let go of her hand to wrap his arm around her shoulders, and she leaned into him, letting his warmth soak into her.

When they reached the pew his family occupied, Joseph nudged Zeb, who offered Ava a smile before turning to tell the rest of the family to make room. They managed to find just enough space for Joseph and Ava. Ava settled against Joseph's side as his father began the service.

Over the past few months, church had begun to feel like a safe place—a place to heal in God's Word. Even so, she sometimes felt like there was still something holding her back. Something keeping her from letting go of the scars on her heart that stopped her from giving it fully to anyone—not to Joseph and not even to God. And she didn't know how to change it.

*Lord, show me how*, she prayed as she sang along to the hymns and listened to the Scripture readings.

When Pastor Calvano moved to the pulpit to deliver the sermon, she slipped her hand into Joseph's. He leaned to give her a quick kiss on the top of her head.

"Children of God," Pastor Calvano started. "Y'all trust me, right?"

Ava glanced around her as heads bobbed. Who wouldn't trust the kind-hearted pastor?

"Good." Pastor Calvano rubbed his hands together in front of him. "So I'm going to pass around a piece of paper, and if you'll just write down any passwords you use. Especially for your bank accounts. Okay?"

There were a few nervous chuckles.

"What?" Pastor Calvano lowered his hands. "You don't trust me enough for that?"

He laughed along with the congregation. "Y'all can stop looking so nervous now. I don't really want your passwords. In fact, you responded exactly like I hoped you would. You got uncomfortable about giving out information that could allow someone to steal your identity. Right? We hear it all the time. Protect your identity. Because lots of identities get stolen every year. And when someone steals your identity, they can do real damage to you."

He paused, letting the words sink in, and Ava could feel the tension in the room build as the congregation waited to see where he was going with this.

"So why is it—" Pastor Calvano's voice went quiet. "That we don't work harder to protect our true identity?"

Ava let out a slow breath. Sometimes she wasn't sure she knew what her true identity was anymore. She used to know—she was the head cheerleader, the model, the pretty one. But now—now she was the broken one.

"To be clear—" Pastor Calvano seemed to look right at her. "When I talk about your true identity, I'm not talking about your name or your Social Security number or even what you do for a living. I'm talking about your identity in Christ."

*Oh.*

"Fortunately, that's not an identity that hackers and thieves are after," Pastor Calvano continued. "But there's a deceiver even more powerful than they are—Satan. And he wants nothing more than to rob you of your identity in Christ. He wants to make you think that your sins are too great for God to forgive. He wants to make you think God's promises aren't for you or even that God's Word isn't the truth. He wants to make you think you are unworthy of love."

Ava sucked in a breath.

*Unworthy of love.* Pastor Calvano's words echoed through her scarred heart. Was that what she felt? Unworthy? Was that what was holding her back?

"And that's not the worst part," Pastor Calvano continued. "The worst part is, he not only tries to steal your identity; he tries to replace it with a new one. He hurls all these new identities at you: broken, unlovable, ugly, stained, marred, despicable, abhorrent. I could keep going . . ."

Ava closed her eyes. Those words—she'd thought every one of them about herself in the past eight years.

No matter how many times Joseph called her beautiful, she still let those other words win out.

"Those words are lies." Pastor Calvano's voice was forceful, and Ava opened her eyes to find Joseph watching her, his face filled with concern.

"Are you all right?" he whispered.

She nodded, pressing her lips together.

She wanted to believe that those words Pastor Calvano had said were lies, but . . .

"Do you know who you are? Do you know your true identity?" Pastor Calvano asked. "Your true identity is as a bride."

Ava's head jerked from Pastor Calvano to Joseph.

He gave her a nervous smile and murmured, "I promise I didn't put him up to that."

"A bride of the great Bridegroom," Pastor Calvano continued. "You know, at a wedding, everyone's focus is on the bride. But I've been to my fair share of weddings over the years, including my son's yesterday."

Ava glanced at Asher, beaming next to his new wife.

"And one thing I can tell you," Pastor Calvano continued, "is that if you want to see someone who's about ready to burst with joy, the person you should be watching is the bridegroom the moment his bride steps through those doors." He gestured to the back of the church, and everyone's heads swiveled that way, as if expecting a bride to be standing there.

Ava pictured the stunning shots she'd gotten of Ireland framed in the doorway yesterday. And then, in spite of her best efforts, she imagined herself standing there, waiting to walk down the aisle to Joseph.

"Isaiah 62:5," Pastor Calvano continued. "As a young man marries a young woman, so will your Builder marry you; as a bridegroom rejoices over his bride, so will your God rejoice over you." His smile traveled around the room. "Can you imagine that? Imagine walking in that door and at the other end of the aisle is God. You're wearing this beautiful white gown that Jesus has given you, and God *rejoices* over you like a bridegroom rejoices over his bride." Pastor Calvano looked toward the ceiling as if he could see it.

Then he shifted his gaze back to the pews. "But see, here's where Satan comes in again. He whispers in your ear, 'Surely God won't rejoice over *you*. You don't deserve that. You're not a beautiful bride, you're wicked, mean, stupid, broken, ugly. You're *unworthy*.'"

"And you know what?" Pastor Calvano shook his head. "He's right. Every one of those things is a reason for God *not* to love you. A reason for him *not* to marry you."

Ava stiffened. That wasn't what he was supposed to say, was it? Wasn't he supposed to tell her that God loved her anyway?

"And yet," Pastor Calvano held up a hand. "He *does* love you. He *rejoices* over you. He makes you his bride. He does this for one reason and one reason alone, and it has nothing to do with you."

He flipped through his Bible. "Ephesians 2:8," he said. "For it is by grace you have been saved, through faith—and this is not from yourselves, it is the gift of God."

Pastor Calvano looked up from the Bible. "Grace. Grace is why God rejoices over us. Why he loves us even though we are unlovable. Why he finds us beautiful even though we are broken. Why he delights in us even though we despise him. His grace makes us lovable. It makes us beautiful. It makes us his brides."

By the time Pastor Calvano closed the sermon, Ava felt like she'd been caught up in a whirlwind. The verses he'd quoted were verses she'd known her whole life.

But somehow, she'd let herself ignore them. She'd let Satan rob her of her true identity as she'd focused on herself. On what she looked like. On how she felt about herself. Instead of on what Christ had done for her. On how he loved her. On how he'd put people in her life who loved her.

She sniffled a few times—but it was no use. The tears refused to be held back. They slipped from her eyes and down her cheeks, probably leaving tracks in the makeup she'd applied so carefully this morning.

But she didn't care.

Because this makeup, the scars it hid—that wasn't her identity.

She'd finally gotten her true identity back.

And she wasn't afraid to let Joseph—or anyone else—see it anymore.

# Chapter 39

Joseph gripped Ava's hand tightly as he drove toward the Children's Hospital. He didn't know what else to do for her.

She'd stopped crying, but she was still quiet, unreadable.

When Dad had mentioned brides in the sermon, Joseph had thought she was going to flee the building. When she'd instead burst into tears and buried her head in his shoulder, he'd held her close and prayed for God's love to wrap around her.

And when she'd finally lifted her head at the end of the service, he'd seen the peace on her face.

*Thank you, Lord, for letting her realize how much you love her. Now please let her see how much I love her and rejoice over her as well.*

He sighed as he pulled into the parking lot of the Children's Hospital.

"You okay?" Ava touched his hand.

"I get to spend the day with the most beautiful woman in the world. How could I not be okay?"

Instead of the look of protest she usually wore when he called her beautiful, Ava smiled and leaned across the console, bringing her lips to his.

He inhaled in surprise but let his hands come to her shoulders, bringing her closer. He'd needed that.

A dog muzzle pressed between them, and they pulled apart, laughing as Griffin turned to lick Joseph's face.

"What was that for?" Joseph asked.

"I think he likes you." Ava patted her dog's head.

Joseph nudged her shoulder. He wasn't going to let her get away with avoiding his question. "I meant *your* kiss. What was that for?"

Ava met his eyes. "To thank you. For not giving up on me. For not letting me push you away."

He held his breath. Was this her way of saying she was ready to accept his proposal?

But Griffin shoved his head between them again.

Joseph patted the dog, then opened his car door.

He'd keep waiting for Ava.

And in the meantime, they had kids inside who shouldn't be kept waiting for their presents.

Ava handed her last gift to a young patient, then glanced across the room, where Joseph and Tasha were delivering a gift to a little boy in a wheelchair.

The box was huge, and Joseph was laughing with the boy, trying to guess what might be in it—but guessing all tiny items, like a stone or a paper clip. The boy was giggling so hard that he started coughing, and Joseph's hand went protectively to the boy's shoulder as he waited for him to catch his breath.

Joseph glanced up, catching Ava's eye and giving her that look she realized now was the same look he'd always given her. Before her scars. And after.

She may have forgotten her identity. But he never had.

"Allie, can I borrow that gift bag?" she asked suddenly, pointing to the small gold bag one of the little girls had gotten. "I'll give it back."

Allie nodded and handed it to her.

"And Sebastian, can I use a piece of paper from your new notebook?"

The boy, who had been drawing in his notebook, nodded, and Ava helped him tear out a sheet.

"Here's a pen." Brianna readjusted her new chemo cap and then passed Ava the gold pen she'd been using to make a card for Wyatt.

"Perfect." Ava took it from her and studied the paper, suddenly at a complete loss.

No words seemed adequate. Until . . .

She scribbled on the paper, folded it in half, and tucked it into the gift bag.

Then she looped the bag on Griffin's collar. "Bring it to Joseph, boy."

She held her breath. The dog had never been given that command before. But maybe in some sort of almost-Christmas miracle, he'd understand it.

*Or not.*

The dog wandered toward a pile of empty wrapping paper in the middle of the floor.

"Griffin," Ava hissed. "Go find Joseph."

Griffin gave her a happy wag, then trotted in the other direction.

"No," several of the kids called, and Griffin stopped, looking confused.

"Go to Joseph," they all shouted.

Griffin turned in a slow circle, then laid down right there in the middle of the room.

Ava groaned. All right then, she was going to have to do this herself.

She retrieved the bag and carried it toward Joseph, who watched her with an amused expression, still crouched next to the boy in the wheelchair.

When she reached him, she held it out silently.

He pushed to his feet. "I thought we were waiting until Christmas for presents."

"Open it." She giggled. She couldn't help it. This felt so perfect. Joseph. Her. The dogs. The kids.

He took the bag from her hand. "It's light." He gave her a teasing look. "Are you giving me an empty bag?"

The kids around them giggled. "Open it," they all called.

Joseph reached into the bag, pulling out the folded up piece of paper. "A mysterious note." He waved it around.

"Read it." Ava appreciated him playing it up for the kids, but she also needed him to hurry up and read what it said.

Slowly, he unfolded the paper. When his eyes fell on the words she'd written, he swallowed and blinked a few times. Then his eyes came to hers.

"Promise?" he whispered.

She nodded, too overcome to say anything.

But she didn't have to. Because Joseph had already swept her up in his arms and caught her lips in his.

As he spun them in a slow circle, the kids cheered and rained balls of wrapping paper onto them.

When they finally pulled apart, Joseph reached into his pocket and pulled out a tiny velvet bag with a silver monogram. A bag Ava hadn't seen in years. Her hands came to her face. She'd known he had a ring, but . . .

"Your Aunt Lori gave this to me." His voice was thick with emotion. "It was your mother's." He tipped the bag to reveal a thin gold band encircled by tiny diamonds. Tears fell onto Ava's hands as Joseph slipped the ring onto her finger. "Forever," he whispered. "My promise is still forever."

# Epilogue

“Smile.” But the photographer’s command was unnecessary. Ava hadn’t stopped smiling once all day. And she was pretty sure she would never stop smiling again.

When she’d stepped into the church an hour ago, she’d kept her eyes on Joseph’s face at the other end of the aisle. She’d savored the light in his eyes, the unstoppable grin on his lips, the way he’d taken a step closer to her even before she’d started down the aisle.

And she’d marveled at what it felt like to be a bride rejoiced over by her bridegroom.

The ceremony had been perfect, with Joseph’s daddy officiating and Aunt Lori, Ava’s matron of honor, sniffling loudly behind her, as Joseph had promised to take Ava for better or for worse, in sickness and in health, till death do them part.

For her part, Ava had been sobbing and laughing at the same time.

“All right, look that way,” the photographer said now, pointing toward the lawn where clusters of guests stood chatting. It was a perfect June day, and no one seemed in a hurry to disperse. She spied Aunt Lori and Michael, who had gotten married only two weeks ago, chatting animatedly with Levi and Grace. And Joseph’s other brothers, roughhousing as usual. And even Madison, wearing a pretty pink dress and helping old Mrs. Talbot to a bench.

“And now look at each other,” the photographer said as she came over to adjust the train of Ava’s wedding dress.

"Gladly," Joseph murmured, and Ava turned to find that his smile matched her own. He tucked the piece of hair that had fallen out of her updo behind her ear, then rested a hand on her bare shoulder. "My beautiful bride."

He'd said it a million times already today, but Ava found she wasn't tired of it yet. Maybe she never would be.

"Um, did you want to turn so your other side is to the camera?" the photographer asked tentatively. Ava had originally told her to get mostly shots of her right side today. She hadn't wanted anything to mar her wedding pictures. Joseph had given her a look when she'd asked but hadn't said anything, for which she was grateful.

But now that today was here, now that she was at her wedding with her wonderful bridegroom who she knew would love her no matter what, she didn't want to hide who she was anymore.

"No," she said. "I'm good like this."

"Yes you are." Joseph lifted a hand to her cheek and lowered his lips to hers as the camera clicked again.

"It should be illegal to be this happy." Ava was still smiling as they got out of the car at Joseph's daddy's—it made her heart glow to think of him as her daddy too now—the next day after church. She and Joseph were leaving for their honeymoon tomorrow, but first they'd wanted to spend one more day with family.

*Family.* The word slipped through her, bringing a glow of joy. She'd never felt like she'd missed out on having a family—Lori had always been there for her, and the Calvanos had felt like family for years already.

But now they really *were* family, officially.

She and Joseph made their way to the backyard, where Pastor Calvano—Daddy—was hard at work over the grill while his children were in various states of conversation or roughhousing.

But the moment they spotted Ava and Joseph, they all started clapping. Zeb was the first to approach them. He held out a hand to shake Joseph's and pulled Ava into a quick hug, saying, "I'm happy for both of you." The rest of the family was close behind with their hugs and congratulations.

When the last one had let them go, Joseph swept an arm under Ava's legs and picked her up, the same way he'd carried her over the threshold of his house—their house—last night. Ava shrieked at being suddenly swept off her feet, but Joseph silenced her with a kiss that made everyone clap again.

Ava was laughing and breathless and oh so happy as Joseph set her back on her feet.

"Food's ready," Daddy called, sounding as happy as Ava felt.

"Before y'all eat," Grace called out. "I have some news."

They all waited as she sucked in an audible breath. "I think I found her. Lydia. Our half-sister."

A hundred questions flew through the air at once but were quickly silenced by Levi's wolf whistle.

"Thank you." Grace smiled at her husband, then continued. "Anyway, I just wanted to let you know that I'm going to try to contact her, and if it's okay with y'all, I'm going to see if she'd be willing to come here to visit. Levi and I will extend our stay, if so."

Grace's gaze scanned the group, pausing on Zeb, who nodded once. Ava let out a breath, glad that her new brothers and sisters seemed to all be on the same page about this.

As the chatter started up again, Ava turned to Joseph. "We should stay too."

Her new husband gaped at her. "Our honeymoon—"

"Will wait." She kissed him. "This is more important. Family is more important."

"Okay." He pulled her to him and kissed her long and slow. "But we're going to take that honeymoon someday soon."

"I promise." Ava rested her head on his chest, savoring this first piece of their forever.

Thanks for reading PIECES OF FOREVER! I hope you loved Joseph and Ava's story! Be sure to grab the next book in the River Falls series, SONGS OF HOME, to find out what happens with the Calvanos' long-lost half-sister, Lydia!

And be sure to sign up for my newsletter to get Asher and Ireland's story, REFLECTIONS OF LOVE, as a free gift. Visit www.valeriembodden.com/freebook to join!

Read on for a preview of SONGS OF HOME...

# A preview of Songs of Home

## Chapter 1

"I'll make you proud," Lydia whispered to the empty outdoor amphitheater. She'd said the same words from every stage before every performance for the past year, though Mama and Daddy would never hear them. The old fear that this would be the time she didn't live up to their legacy gripped her around the gut, and she tried to ignore it. But it was harder today than usual. Maybe because it was her birthday? And for the first time in forty years, her parents wouldn't be here to say they loved her.

Lydia peeled a sticky lock of hair off her neck—the Nashville humidity was brutal today, just as she'd warned Dallas it would be when he'd scheduled this tour stop. She supposed she should be grateful—at least she'd get to sleep in her own bed tonight. With a muttered, "happy birthday" to herself, she made her way backstage, trying to shake off the unsuitable melancholy. It was her birthday, she was on the last leg of what so far had been a massively successful national tour—one poised to launch her and Dallas to the levels of fame Mama and Daddy had achieved—and she was in love.

With a man she hadn't seen since their sound check a few hours ago.

Maybe he was preparing a surprise for her. A tingle went up her spine. Maybe the surprise would be a ring.

She pushed the thought away. Just because they'd been dating for a few years didn't mean Dallas had to propose. He would do it when he was ready—and she wouldn't pressure him. Though he *had* been acting different lately—kind of nervous. And he'd said something about things changing the other day that had made her think that . . . maybe.

She shook off the hope.

At any rate, there wouldn't be time for him to do it before the concert—she had her hair and makeup to do yet, not to mention squeezing herself into the silver dress Cheyenne had insisted would be perfect for tonight's concert. Lydia cringed just imagining trying to pull it on. She loved that her best friend was also her backup vocalist and guitarist, but maybe she should replace her as fashion adviser. Eight years younger than Lydia, Cheyenne might still be able to get away with wearing tight sequined dresses. But Lydia was starting to feel ridiculous in them.

*What if he did it on stage?* The question filtered through her thoughts. She pressed her hands to her cheeks, which suddenly felt too warm.

*Stop it. You don't even know he's going to do it at all.*

But she knew who probably did know: Cheyenne. Somehow, the woman was the first to know every piece of gossip that floated through the band, the crew, even the audience sometimes.

She rushed for the dressing room, determined to find out what her best friend knew. It might ruin the surprise, but her nerves were already frayed to the point of breaking after the exhaustion of three months on the road.

The door stuck, but she shoved hard and it opened. “Hey Chey, do you think—”

Her words got caught in her chest as she grabbed for the door frame. A wave of dizziness nearly knocked her to the ground.

She couldn’t make sense of what she was seeing.

A woman with a blonde braid hanging to her waist. A man with a shaggy mop of dark hair.

She couldn’t see much else since their lips were pressed together, their arms locked around each other.

*Kissing*. The word swam at her through the fog, smacking her in the face with a cold splash.

“Dallas. What are you— I don’t— Cheyenne.” She had to stop to gasp for air. Who had sucked all the oxygen out of the room?

Cheyenne jumped back from Dallas with a quiet shriek. His reaction was less pronounced, a calm turn and a grimace.

“I don’t— What are—” Lydia tried again, blinking a few times as if that would change the frame frozen in front of her.

“Lydia—” Cheyenne’s hands were on her lips, as if she could hide the evidence of what she’d been doing. “This isn’t what it looks like.” But the guilt in her best friend’s eyes didn’t lie.

“Actually—” Dallas stepped forward. “It is. I’m sorry, Lydia. I wanted to wait until after the tour. But maybe it’s best if you know now. Cheyenne and I are . . .” He looked at Cheyenne, and Lydia could already tell.

“In love,” she filled in dully. How, oh how, had she not seen it before? All those nights she’d gone to bed early and they’d stayed up to “work on songs.” All those tour stops where she went for a walk alone, only to get back to the bus and find the two of them gone. All the time Cheyenne spent gushing to her about how great Dallas was.

"This doesn't change anything, Lydia." Cheyenne reached for her, but Lydia took a step backward.

Didn't change anything?

It blew up her whole life.

Again.

The only two people she had left in the world were saying they had chosen each other over her.

"I know this isn't ideal." Dallas took a step toward her, and she snorted. Not ideal was having a show on her birthday. Not ideal was squeezing into a dress she could barely breathe in. Not ideal was the humidity that would slick her in sweat the moment she stepped onto the stage.

But this?

This was way beyond not ideal.

"But," Dallas continued. "We have appearances to keep up here. This isn't the time to fall apart."

Lydia blinked at him. "Who's falling apart?" She steeled her spine, same way she had for every show since Mama and Daddy's deaths. She shoved down the urge to run out of the amphitheater and never look back. That wasn't an option.

Instead, she kept her shoulders stiff, lifted her head higher, and skirted around Dallas and Cheyenne to grab her dress and makeup bag. Then, without a word, she made her way back into the hall and down to the ladies' room. For tonight, this would be her dressing room.

By the time she'd gotten ready, an appealing numbness had settled over her. As long as she didn't have to see Dallas and Cheyenne, didn't have to talk to them, she could put herself in a little bubble and pretend none of what had just happened was real. At least until the concert was over.

But the moment she emerged from the bathroom, Cheyenne pounced at her. "Lydia, I really think—"

Lydia spun on her heel and burst back through the bathroom door. She dove into the first stall, ducking over the toilet just in time to avoid vomiting on her glittery cowboy boots.

When she was done, she wiped her face, flushed, and stepped out of the stall to wash her hands and rinse her mouth.

She'd half-expected Cheyenne to be there, holding out a paper towel as she had at every show, making the same stupid joke she made every time about how much Lydia's vomit would be worth on the internet. But the bathroom was empty, and when she emerged, so was the hallway.

She let out a long, slow breath. She'd seen her parents perform through the flu, a massive tabloid uproar, and even appendicitis. She was going to get through this concert and make them proud of her tonight if it killed her. There'd be time to deal with her emotions later.

Dallas and Cheyenne were in the wings, Cheyenne holding Dallas's arm and whispering earnestly. She cut off abruptly as Lydia approached.

"Thirty seconds," a panicked looking stage manager said, pressing Lydia's mic into her hand.

"Give us a minute." Dallas's low rumble held a command Lydia had never seen anyone ignore.

She smoothed a hand down her dress. "We don't need a minute."

"Lydia, I think we should–" Cheyenne started. But the stage manager was waving them onto the stage.

Dallas's hand grabbed Lydia's, and the shock of his touch almost drew tears. She needed to avoid contact if she wanted to keep this bubble around her.

But he squeezed tighter and leaned toward her, his hot breath brushing over her ear. "As far as these people know, we're supposed to be in love. That's what they came to see."

"Yeah," Lydia murmured. "We're supposed to be."

And then they were on the stage, the lights dazzling, the crowd cheering, the music beating. Lydia tugged her hand out of Dallas's and ignored the choreography they'd rehearsed, instead letting herself get caught up in the rhythm of the song. She stepped to the front of the stage to touch fans' hands, something she usually avoided. Lights flashed brilliantly over her, and she let herself get sucked into the magic that was the show.

She could get through this.

And she almost did.

But as the lights lowered and the music slowed for the final set of the evening, Dallas moved to her side, sliding an arm behind her back, as the choreography called for him to do.

Lydia attempted to slip away, but his grip tightened and he leaned over to whisper in her ear, "Personal problems aside, you know that."

When he pulled away, he offered her an intimate smile that she knew was entirely for the benefit of the crowd.

She tensed as his deep baritone with its light twang carried the first notes of the song:

*Once upon a time, I promised you forever,*
*But darling, I didn't mean what I said.*
*Because forever would never be enough*
*To show you every ounce of my love.*
*So tonight, let me make a new promise, hon:*
*Tonight I promise you forever plus one.*

She slipped out of his grip. But she could feel his eyes on her, feel the sigh of the crowd, feel the light wisp of wind on her sweaty back.

She forced herself to turn her head toward him like she was supposed to and drew in a shaky breath. But when she opened her mouth to begin her verse, her usually rich alto broke on the first note, and a painfully loud sob reverberated through the mic.

Slapping a hand to her mouth to hold the rest of her cries back, she chucked her microphone, noting with a detached sort of satisfaction that Dallas had to step aside to avoid getting hit. She spun on the heels of her cowboy boots and sprinted for the wings, humiliation hot on her heels.

As she fled down the hallway, she heard Cheyenne's voice take up her part, and it hit her—the song had probably been meant for Cheyenne all along.

A fresh wave of desperation and adrenaline drove her straight toward the exit.

## Chapter 2

Liam leaned against the front of his van, head tilted toward the dark sky, watching the play of lights from the other side of the amphitheater reflecting off the clouds. He'd finished the job, finished packing his gear into the van, and yet he couldn't make himself get in and drive away. This was his last night in Nashville, and he felt an overpowering need to soak it all in.

The city held some of the best memories of his life—the years with his wife, the birth of their daughter Mia, and the fast-paced adrenaline of setting up the lighting for shows like this one.

Life in his hometown of River Falls would be nothing like this, he knew that. But what choice did he have? After her fall, Mama needed him to help care for the house, and he needed to get Mia away from the bad crowd she'd fallen in with—especially that delinquent of a boyfriend. If that meant a three-hour move away from everything he'd come to love over the past twenty years, then so be it. He'd promised Molly he'd do whatever it took to make sure Mia never drifted from the faith—and right now he was failing miserably at that. Actually, it felt like he'd been failing miserably at everything when it came to parenting for the past year or more.

"I sure wish you were here to help me figure this out," he murmured into the dark, unable to keep himself from talking to his wife even six years after her death.

The sound of pounding footsteps yanked his gaze to the path that ran from the amphitheater to the parking lot. A woman in a silver dress barreled toward him at full speed, jerking to a stop at the last second as her eyes landed on him. She let out a small, low-pitched squawk, staring at him with wild eyes, black makeup lines streaking her wet cheeks.

Something about the brokenness in her gaze tugged at his heart, and he pushed off the van to step toward her.

She squawked again but seemed unable to move.

"Are you okay?" He kept his voice gentle. "Can I get you some help?"

She shook her head but didn't move, and he took a step closer. "Are you sure? Maybe I could call someone for you? The police or . . . someone."

She lifted her hands to her cheeks, spreading the streaks of makeup all the way to her hairline, her eyes roving the parking lot as if searching for her car.

"Actually—" Her voice was deeper than he'd expected, resonant and warm. Almost like the cello his wife used to play. "I could use a ride."

He pulled out his phone. "I'll call a taxi for you."

But she gave him a desperate look. "I can't wait for a taxi. I need to get out of here right now."

"Why? Are you sure I can't call the police?" He peered behind her. He didn't see any signs of anyone chasing her. Maybe she was running *from* the police.

"Not unless they can arrest a cheating jerk and my best friend." She sniffed but managed the smallest grimace of a smile.

"Ah." A protective instinct flared in his chest, and he took a step closer to the building, then stopped himself. What was he going to do, deck a guy he'd never met?

"Look. I know this is a lot to ask. But could you give me a ride? I rode here with said jerk and friend." The woman turned her eyes on him. Where Molly's had been a light, sparkling blue and full of laughter, this woman's were as deep and full and soulful as her voice. And yet they seemed to have an equivalent effect on him—a desire to shield her.

"You're not really asking a complete stranger for a ride, are you? Because that isn't exactly a safe thing to do. For all you know, I could be a serial killer or a kidnapper or a . . . a litterer."

The woman managed a small laugh. "I'll take my chances. Besides, I can tell you're a good guy. You've probably never littered in your life. Come on." The woman moved toward the passenger door of the van bearing the logo of his electrical company. "I'll pay you. A thousand dollars. Please."

"I don't want your money."

But the woman was already opening the door and climbing into the van.

Liam blew out a hard breath. He knew he wouldn't hurt her. But *she* didn't know that. He really shouldn't let her . . . But if he didn't give her a ride, someone else might. Someone with less innocent intentions.

"Fine." He opened the driver's door to find the woman huddled in the passenger seat, wiping at her eyes again. "You're sure you're all right?"

She nodded with a loud sniffle. "Sorry. I'm fine." She gave him her address, then leaned her head against her seat.

Liam backed out of his parking spot and navigated into the street, trying to keep from looking at her too often—and failing miserably. Her silver dress was glittery, her boots even more so—but that wasn't what kept drawing his eyes to her. It wasn't even the natural beauty he could discern under her streaked makeup. It was the sense of familiarity he got looking at her. But for the life of him, he couldn't place it.

"You don't like music?" The woman's voice broke into the silence.

"I— What makes you say that?"

"You don't have the radio on," she pointed out.

"Oh." Aside from hymns in church, Liam avoided music as much as he could these days. It held too many memories of Molly. "You can turn it on if you want."

"I'm not the biggest fan of music at the moment either." The woman's laugh was sharp, before she fell into silence. After a few minutes, her eyes closed, and Liam took it as a sign that she wasn't interested in talking.

They drove the rest of the way like that, until Liam pulled into the driveway at the address she'd given him. He couldn't help letting out a low whistle as he drove past the sprawling, perfectly manicured lawn toward a brick home fronted by tall white columns. A place this big could only be called a mansion.

He cut off his whistle as he realized it probably wasn't the most sophisticated thing to do. His gaze slipped to the woman, but she hadn't opened her eyes.

In that case . . . He gaped openly, noting the full wraparound porch and the bubbling fountain and the tropical-looking flower beds.

Who *was* this woman?

He slowed the van to a stop alongside the house, then turned to her to say . . . Well, he wasn't sure what to say. "Goodnight" or "good luck" or "your boyfriend was clearly an idiot." But her eyes were still closed, and her lips were parted the smallest crack, moving slightly as tiny puffs of air slipped out of them. A faint pulse went through his heart as he watched her, the tiniest sign of life where there had been only a dead circuit for the past six years.

He ignored it.

He had no desire for his heart to come back to life—not without Molly.

He cleared his throat, hoping that would be enough to wake the woman in the passenger seat. When it wasn't, he touched a hand to her shoulder, ignoring its soft warmth as he shook her gently.

But she still didn't stir.

He eyed the walkway from the driveway to her front door. He supposed he could carry her, but what would he do once he got her to the door? Break in so he could set her down?

Fortunately, the moment he took his hand off her shoulder, her eyes popped open. She gasped, looking around wildly and reaching for the door.

"It's okay." He kept his voice low so as not to startle her further. "You fell asleep. But we're here."

Clarity came back to the woman's eyes as they fell on him. "See, I told you that you're a good guy."

He frowned. "It's a good thing too."

She nodded, her eyes meeting his. Something in the air between them sparked to life, something Liam felt right down to that new pulse in his heart.

He looked away.

"Oh, let me get you your money." The woman pushed her door open.

"I don't want your money. Really. Just—"

The woman blinked at him. "Just what?"

"Are you going to be okay?" It probably shouldn't matter to him, but it did.

"You must think I'm crazy." Though she delivered the words with a laugh, there was a certain vulnerability behind them.

He let his eyes flick to her, offering a small smile. "A little, maybe. But crazy isn't always such a bad thing."

Her laugh was edged with regret. She got out of the van but didn't close the door. "At least let me offer you some sweet tea as a thank you. And some cake. It's my birthday." Her lips twisted with irony.

Oh man. Her boyfriend had cheated on her on her birthday?

*Go home.* He had a lot to do yet tonight to make sure everything was ready for the movers tomorrow.

But how could he make her eat birthday cake alone? "All right." He reached for his door handle. "But only a slice."

He followed her to the backyard, which felt cozy and secluded despite the imposing house.

"Have a seat." The woman gestured to the cushy patio set under a wooden pergola. "I'm going to run in and make some tea." She disappeared into the house, and Liam lowered himself onto the patio couch, trying to pretend her smile wasn't still zapping through his veins. He was leaving tomorrow and would never see this woman again. Which, given the way his heart seemed to be attempting to jump-start itself, was probably a good thing.

He tilted his head back to peer through the slats of the pergola above him. Was this the same sky he'd been looking at half an hour ago when this woman—he realized he hadn't asked her name—had crashed into his life?

The clouds from earlier had cleared, and millions of lights twinkled down at him. He picked out Virgo, which had always been Molly's favorite constellation because she said it looked like someone playing a cello. He'd never been able to see the resemblance, but he'd loved her passion in describing it to him.

With a start, he brought his gaze back down to earth.

What was he doing here?

After six years of barely so much as speaking to a woman outside of work contexts, he was sitting in the backyard of some strange—beautiful, granted, but strange—woman's house.

He pushed to his feet. If he left now, he wouldn't have to explain why it was a bad idea for him to be here.

But then he pictured the tears that had streaked her face as she'd run toward his van earlier. She'd already been hurt once tonight. He couldn't do that to her again.

He'd wait for her to come outside, apologize, and then go home.

Go home and not think about her again.

Just like he wasn't thinking about her right now.

The moment he heard the door open, he sprang to his feet. "Look, I should—"

"I wasn't sure if you liked frosting or not. So I brought one piece with lots and one with a little. You choose." She'd changed into jeans and a loose-fitting t-shirt, and her hair fell around her shoulders in thick, dark waves. She'd washed the streaks of makeup off her face, and her eyes were warm and bright.

And Liam completely forgot what he'd been about to say.

"I'll take the one with less frosting," he finally stammered, waiting until she'd set the tray of tea and cake down and taken a seat to sit as well.

She poured the tea into glasses, then handed him one. He took it, careful not to let his fingers brush hers. He'd eat a slice of cake and *then* go.

"This is an amazing place." Liam eyed the giant house as he took a bite of the cake, the perfect blend of fluffy and sweet mingling on his tongue.

"Thanks." She scooped a bite of cake—complete with a giant frosting flower—into her mouth, a streak of purple dotting her lips as she brought her fork down.

Liam was seized by the oddest urge to wipe it away, but fortunately she picked up a napkin and rubbed her lips before he could do something stupid. He directed his eyes to his plate, studying his cake so he could get his thoughts under control.

"It's ridiculously big for me. I think I use like three rooms." She set her cake down to sip her tea.

"You live in this big place by yourself?" He cringed as he heard how the question must have sounded. "I mean—"

But she laughed gently. "It was my parents'. They left it to me when they died."

*Nice one, Liam.*

"I'm so sorry." He couldn't stop himself from touching her hand. But the jolt to his middle made him pull back immediately.

The woman didn't seem to notice. "I should probably sell it. But I'm not quite ready yet."

Liam nodded, resisting the urge to wrap his hand protectively around hers. He knew too well how hard it was to let go of a place that held so many memories.

"Anyway." She seemed to chase away the thoughts. "What about you? You live in Nashville?"

"Until tomorrow. We're moving back to my hometown." He sighed as a thousand images of his life hit him at once. "I'm going to miss it here. Lots of good memories."

She gave him a bemused look. "I think about leaving sometimes. But I don't know where I would go."

He had a crazy urge to invite her to come to River Falls. Fortunately, his mouth was full of cake, and by the time he'd swallowed it, his common sense had returned. “I love Nashville. My wife and I came here for college and never left. But—”

“Your wife.” The woman looked horrified. “I’m so sorry. I didn’t mean to keep you from being with your family on your last night in town. You should go.” She reached for his plate, but he switched it to his other hand.

“My wife died. Six years ago.”

The horror in the woman’s eyes transformed to compassion. “I’m sorry. That must have been so devastating.”

His eyes went to hers, and he could tell it wasn’t a platitude. She hadn’t said it because it was expected. She’d experienced it too.

“Yeah.” He cleared his throat. “My daughter Mia has been struggling, and I think I need to get her out of the city. Plus my mama fell and needs some help, so . . .”

“I’m sure your hometown isn’t such a bad place.” She settled back into the couch, as if she planned for him to stay and chat a while.

“It’s not. It’s where Molly and I met, actually. I only hope I’m doing the right thing for Mia.”

The woman frowned. “I’m sure you are. How old is she?”

“Sixteen. I don’t know what happened.” He set his empty plate down, and the next thing he knew, he was telling her about Mia and about Mama and even about Molly.

Whenever he tried to direct the conversation toward her, she deflected.

Finally, they fell silent and the woman covered a giant yawn with her hand. Though it had to be well past midnight, Liam wasn’t tired in the least. But he should let the poor woman get some sleep.

Regretfully, he got to his feet. It felt like an invisible tether had woven between them over the past couple hours, and he was reluctant to break it.

"Thanks for the tea and cake." He gestured toward the table with the empty dishes, then tucked his hands in his pockets. "This was . . ."

"Surreal?" The woman's smile was sweet and a little wistful as she stood too.

He chuckled. "Surreal but nice."

"Yes it was. Thank you for being a good guy." She stepped forward and, before he could react, dropped a quick kiss on his cheek.

His hand lifted involuntarily to the spot, the pulse in his heart strengthening into a full-out throb.

"I don't even know your name." Not that it mattered at this point. He would never see her again.

"Maybe it's better that way." Her throaty whisper curled around him, making him want to sit back down, but he nodded and took a step backward.

"Maybe it is." He made his feet turn and carry him toward his van. When he reached it, he peered into the backyard, but there was no sign of the woman.

With a sigh, he ran his hand over his cheek.

He might never see this woman again—but he wasn't likely to forget her anytime soon.

## The River Falls Series

While the books in the River Falls series are linked, each is a complete romance featuring a different couple.

Pieces of Forever (Joseph & Ava)
Songs of Home (Lydia & Liam)
Memories of the Heart (Simeon & Abigail)
Whispers of Truth (Benjamin & Summer)

## River Falls Christmas Romances

Wondering about some of the side characters in River Falls who aren't members of the Calvano family? Join them as they get their own happily-ever-afters in the River Falls Christmas Romances.

Christmas of Joy

## The Hope Springs Series

While the books in the Hope Springs series are linked, each is a complete romance featuring a different couple.

Not Until Christmas (Ethan & Ariana)
Not Until Forever (Sophie & Spencer)
Not Until This Moment (Jared & Peyton)
Not Until You (Nate & Violet)
Not Until Us (Dan & Jade)
Not Until Christmas Morning (Leah & Austin)
Not Until This Day (Tyler & Isabel)
Not Until Someday (Grace & Levi)
Not Until Now (Cam & Kayla)
Not Until Then (Bethany & James)
Not Until The End (Emma & Owen)

## Want to know when my next book releases?

You can follow me on Amazon to be the first to know when my next book releases! Just visit amazon.com/author/valeriembodden and click the follow button.

# Acknowledgements

Whether our scars are visible or invisible, I think we all carry some of Ava in us. Some of that fear that we are unworthy and there is no reason for anyone—let alone God—to love us. And yet, God's message to us is the same as his message to Ava—he loves us even though we are unworthy. He loves us so much that he sent his Son to die for our sins and to make us worthy. For that—and for the awesome privilege of sharing that great good news—I thank him every day.

You know, every time I write my acknowledgements, I feel a little bit like Ava, in complete awe of all the people God has put into my life who show me his love every day. I thank him for blessing me with an amazing, supportive, all-around-wonderful husband and four incredible, creative, Jesus-loving children. As much as I love the time I spend with my imaginary friends from River Falls, I love and treasure time with the five of you even more. You bring joy and laughter and pure delight to my life.

I also thank God for all the people in my life who I may not see every day but who I know are rooting for me and encouraging me just the same: my parents and sister, in-laws, extended family, friends, and even people I've never met in person. What a blessing!

And while I'm thanking God, I have to offer an extra warm thanks for my advance reader team, who offered their wise feedback and insights on Ava and Joseph's story: Jessica Koeser, Michelle M., Vickie, Judy L., Swtkapoor, Sandy Golinger, Jenny M., Jennifer Ellenson, Karen Jernigan, Jean S., Ilona, Jenny Kilgallen, Trista Heuer, Rhondia Cannon, Melanie Tate, Pat, Chinye, Becky Collins, Sandy H. Mary S., Terri Camp, Seyi A., Jan Gilmour, Aurélie Detampel, Lincoln Clark, Bonny Rambarran, Trudy Cordle, Mary Tanner, Vickie Escalante, Carol Brandon, Shelia Garrison, Korkoi

Boret, Ann M. Diener, Pam Williams, Margaret N., Kris Boardman, Barb Frey, Paula Hurdle, Judith, Sharon, Patty Bohuslav, NJM, Jeanne Olynick, Karen Bonner, Connie, Kellie P., Gary L. Richards, Alison K., Vikki, Teresa M., Bobbie McCord, Kelly Wickham, Connie Gandy, Kori Thomas, Deb Galloway, Karalee, Jaime Fipp, Karen, Becky C., Barb Miller, Tonya, and Kvee.

And finally, I thank God for you! Thank you for spending time with these characters I've grown to love. I hope they've found a place in your heart—and more importantly that you've been reminded of your place in God's heart and your identity as his bride. God's blessings to you!

# About the Author

Valerie M. Bodden has three great loves: Jesus, her family, and books. And chocolate (okay, four great loves). She is living out her happily ever after with her high-school-sweetheart-turned-husband and their four children. Her life wouldn't make a terribly exciting book, as it has a happy beginning and middle, and someday when she goes to her heavenly home, it will have a happy end.

She was born and raised in Wisconsin but recently moved with her family to Texas, where they're all getting used to the warm weather (she doesn't miss the snow even a little bit, though the rest of the family does) and saying y'all instead of you guys.

Valerie writes emotion-filled Christian fiction that weaves real-life problems, real-life people, and real-life faith. Her characters may (okay, will) experience some heartache along the way, but she will always give them a happy ending.

Feel free to stop by www.valeriembodden.com to say hi. She loves visitors! And while you're there, you can sign up for your free book.

Printed in Great Britain
by Amazon

38135638R00148